Chokecherry Girl

A NOVEL

by

Barbara Meyer Link

FROM THE TINY ACORN ...
GROWS THE MIGHTY OAK

Chokecherry Girl

First Edition

Book interior design and digital formatting by Debra Cranfield Kennedy.

https://commons.wikimedia.org/wiki/File:Chevrolet_Bel_Air_Convertible_1957_(14193443053).jpg

www.acornpublishingllc.com

ISBN—Hardcover 978-1-952112-19-5
ISBN—Paperback 978-1-952112-18-8
Library of Congress Control Number: 2020920585

For all my fellow writers,
may they have the joy of seeing
their beautiful words in print.

Chapter One

1958

The worst thing about babysitting for the O'Malley's was the dead baby. When the bell rang at their mortuary next door, Bobbi would leave the kids and unlock the door so family and friends could view the deceased.

There she was, the silent baby tucked into a satin-lined box like a doll under the Christmas tree. Her tiny hands remained fixed in place, pointing to nothing or maybe to heaven.

For other baby-sitting dangers, Bobbi devised a strategy. After all, in 1958 she was a freshman in high school and knew a few things. So when dads drove her home, she scooted to the far side of the front seat. If any of them grabbed her, she'd pull Grandma's darning needle from her sleeve and jam it into his arm.

You'd be surprised how many husbands tried to feel her up. The men left home in ironed white shirts with clean-shaven cheeks smelling of Old Spice and talking in company voices. But during the evening, they grew stubble, breathed liquor fumes and pawed at a flat-chested fourteen-year-old girl.

1958. The year in which Bobbi tangled with the adults—Patsy, the beautician; Mary Agnes, the Crow Indian; and Miss Bauer, the new teacher. Bobbi knew she should have obeyed the law and her parents. She never thought it crucial until she stood before the judge.

"Donna," she'd said to her best friend, "honestly, I wanted to kneel with prayer hands like the picture of Jesus in the Garden of Gethsemane, maybe with the Platters playing 'My Prayer' in the background. Not because it was religious, but because it sounded sad and romantic. Dad said no! No kneeling and no music in Judge Henderson's chambers."

"I love the Platters! That would have been so cool," Donna said.

"No shit," Bobbi replied.

The trouble started the first week of March when she discovered the car parked behind the high school. A '57 black Chevy convertible with red leather seats, slick red steering wheel, acres of polished chrome, and white wall tires like frosted donuts. A black and red shining jewel.

Bobbi rode to school that day with her dad. He looked uncool in his khaki pants and sweatshirt. He was the high school basketball coach, so he didn't dress up. His clothes looked like they'd been in the ironing basket for a month. Once she even spotted his jockstrap peeking over his grody sweatpants.

From behind the school, they had a clear view of a new business— a beauty shop in an old house trailer. The blonde beautician stood in her doorway, smoking and staring at them like they were something to see.

Bobbi felt like yelling, "Take a picture, it'll last longer."

Dad glanced at the blonde, and then entered the school through the back door. Bobbi paused by the Black Beauty, smoothed her hand over the hood, inhaled the fragrance of the high gloss wax and felt the sun-soaked shiny metal.

A young woman stepped out of the school's back door and lit a cig. Her seeking eyes peered from heavy-framed black glasses. Her short dark hair looked pushed in place, not brushed. She wore a rumpled tweed skirt, white Oxford shirt, and penny loafers. Altogether, she gave off a quality of intensity, beyond her lean, muscular build.

Bobbi knew all of the instructors, so she assumed this must be the new English teacher. A huge improvement over old lady Schumann who reeked of mothballs and had broken her hip.

"My new rag top. Like it?" the woman asked.

Bobbi sucked in a lungful of air. She'd never ridden in a convertible! "Very cool," she stammered, hoping she wouldn't pee her pants.

The teacher displayed a faint expression on her lips, something stealthy, a smile that was not a smile. She tossed her cigarette and went back inside the school.

Bobbi raced to the girl's can to meet Donna and Rita. Since second grade, they'd been tight. She set her books on the edge of the rusty sink and glanced in the mirror. The bathroom's slick green walls made her complexion look like pond water.

"I'm not kidding," she exclaimed as she combed her thick eyebrows. "The new English sub drives a convertible with California plates. You've got to see it! Jesus God, I could drive to San Francisco in that car!"

"Like that's going to ever happen," Rita said. "Your crinoline is showing."

She pulled her net petticoat up at the waist, and rolled it over twice. "Is that better?"

"Yes." Donna unwrapped a piece of Bazooka bubble gum and read the comic strip inside. "'Where do you find your boyfriend's heart?'"

"Where?" Bobbi asked. "None of us even have boyfriends!"

Donna giggled. "'In the Tunnel of Love.'"

"Oh, brother! Seriously, why would a sub want to teach in Bowman, Montana?" Rita stretched her gum in a long pink string, and then tucked it back into her mouth. "Criminy, we're stuck out here on the prairie, only three thousand people in the whole county."

"I checked the booklist for her class. It's J. D. Salinger," Bobbi paused for full effect, "and he's America's most reclusive author!"

"Like using big words will get you a date, nerd," Rita sneered. "It's all so stupid, anyway. I'd rather read a movie magazine." She pulled her angora sweater over the lumpy mounds on her chest.

"For your information, Salinger's book is on the 'Adults Only' shelf at the library." Bobbi blotted her lipstick on a piece of toilet paper. "It's all about adolescent angst."

"Only a geek knows that."

Bobbi pushed open the heavy door. "No, only a geek stuffs Kleenex in her bra. Later, gator."

Donna and Bobbi sat on Bobbi's bed. They sucked toothpicks soaked in cinnamon oil. Then they put their feet sole to sole and bicycled. They were in harmony, even when they put each other down. It was Friday night, and they glued their ears to radio Request Time, hoping *they'd* get a dedication.

"Did you notice my pink chenille bedspread?" Bobbi asked.

"I'm sitting on it, dummy. It's cool, and I dig the way you taped up pictures of the stars."

"I cut them out of *Silver Screen*. The one of Sandra Dee is an actual signed picture."

Donna sighed. "She's so ginchy."

"Cast your eyeballs on this." Bobbi flapped a paper. "This is what I wanted to tell you. January was zip. I heard *no* headboard banging."

"You can hear your parents doing it?"

"This is my chart. The time is in red, and the dates in blue."

"You're so weird!"

"It's a scientific study. Their average time is twenty minutes. Nothing in January or February."

"Jeez Louise, I can make out for hours." Donna shook the nail polish bottle. "Do you like this color? Dripping Fuchsia, Sandra Dee's choice. Oh, turn up the radio. It's the Everly Brothers. 'Wake up Little Susie.' Can you imagine staying out all night? Wouldn't you just die if you got caught?"

"So what do you think is wrong with my parents?"

"Maybe they're just quiet. I never hear my folks. I think they do it when they send us to the Saturday matinee."

"During the *day*?" Bobbi breathed her amazement.

"Shut up about doing it. I swear it's all you talk about. Here's Request Time."

They listened to the dedications and requests. "Come Go With Me," for Hazel, a cute cheerleader. "A White Sport Coat," for Marlene, Bobbi's older sister.

Bobbi grabbed her heart pillow and danced around the room. She pursed her lips to kiss the pillow then listened to the next request. "Skinny Minnie," for Bobbi Vernon from Melvin.

"Shit, double shit." Bobbi's ears got as pink as the bedspread. "Melvin—there's no Melvin in our class." She threw the pillow at the radio. It missed and thudded against the wall. Picking it up, she threw it harder. The radio took a direct hit and crashed to the floor.

Donna tossed a wad of cotton back at Bobbi. "Don't go apeshit!"

"What do you care?" Bobbi righted the radio. "You actually have a butt. No one's going to call you skinny on the radio."

All weekend she heard "Skinny Minnie" in her head. And she had two bad dreams about the dead baby.

On Saturday, she locked the bathroom door and gave herself the once over in the mirror. At five feet nine inches, she towered above her sister and friends. She often slouched and heard her mother whisper to Mag, "She's too tall. Should have been a boy."

Her hair was a medium brown, like the neighbor's spaniel, and her eyes were hazel, just another word for brown. Her neck was long. It seemed twice the normal amount of neck. Standing on the bathtub rim, she scrutinized her figure. The seat of her pants folded in instead of curving out. Shit. Too skinny and too brown.

The song in her head changed to, "Poor Little Fool."

Bobbi dreaded going to school on Monday, afraid a kid would call her *Skinny Minnie*. On Sunday she called long distance to Minnesota.

"Grandma, can I come and live with you? I'll wash the canning jars and pull the dandelions. I'll shuffle the cards when we play Canasta." She already knew the answer.

Here's the way Bobbi saw the solar system. Adults lived on their own planet. The men had jobs Monday through Friday and the women had ironing, casserole recipes, and bridge parties. On Saturday night the couples got together for duck dinners in the winter, and cookouts in the summer. After which there was a lot of headboard banging. Parents didn't care what their kids did as long as they did it quietly and didn't bother them. The teens lived on their own planet, which consisted of school, rock and roll, cars, the neat kids and the creeps. Bobbi wasn't one of the *neats*.

Chapter Two

M ary Agnes Lone Hill had Belafonte on the hi-fi. He was the hot new singing sensation with his chocolate voice and brilliant white teeth. His '56 *Calypso* album was the latest sound.

She did a kind of push dance, what the Crow Indians called a foxtrot, with the vacuum over the new wall-to-wall carpet. Mrs. Henderson had said White Grapes was the official carpet color. Mary Agnes worked over the traffic areas until her ponytail came loose and her man's shirt swirled around her legs and she could smell her own armpits.

She turned her back to her image, which was reflected in the picture window. She wasn't proud of her looks. Short and squat, she was low to the ground like a well-built fence. Her coarse black hair framed a flat face the color of copper pennies, and her nose curved slightly to the left side of her face after it was broken in a drunken tumble.

"*Day-Oh, Daaay-Oh. Daylight come and I want to go home,*" she sang along with Harry. With each step, she worked up her courage. Pretty Weasel needed a helping hand—she *had* to ask today.

Mrs. Henderson, her employer, unexpectedly touched her arm.

"Mary Agnes, are you playing my new record?"

"Yes, Ma'am," she said, trying to sound obedient. She had lost her job at the dry cleaners and really needed this one. "I'm real careful. I did the sheets just like you showed me—folded the corners so they look nice and neat in the linen closet."

"Good." Mrs. Henderson held a history book. "Look at these Indians on a Montana hill."

Mary Agnes examined the picture. The men rode bareback with war bonnets, buckskin leggings and feather-decorated lances. Ochre and black stripes adorned their stern, handsome faces. Their fine horses possessed similar markings around their eyes and flanks. It could have been a scene from a Hollywood movie. The caption read "Great Plains Indians, 1896."

"These are your people, real Indians. Mary Agnes, you should be proud of your heritage."

"Yes, Ma'am."

"Are you about finished?" Mrs. Henderson asked. "I've got to get to the beauty shop."

"Are you going to see the coach's wife? Can you ask her about my boy?" She tucked in her shirttail. "He's crazy for basketball. I need to help him make the team."

She put her hands on her maid's shoulders. "Why, Mary Agnes Lone Hill, you've never mentioned him. I didn't know you had a child." She leaned in close. "Have you been drinking?"

"No, Ma'am. My boy is Donald Pretty Weasel. He's sixteen and lives with my cousin, his 'other mother.'"

"Is he in school?" She glanced at her watch. "I'll mention it to Lois, Coach Vernon's wife. I'm sure we can do something for him, if he's good. Pretty Weasel, that's his name?"

Mary Agnes was excited. If she did him a favor, he might let her back into his life. Over the years, she'd missed him so much.

She hurried to empty the wastebaskets and do the beds in the children's rooms. The sheets were pink for the two girls and blue for the three boys. The new contour sheets were the first she'd seen, and they made bed-making easy. She thought of the bare mattress in her tarpaper shack.

Yes, Mrs. Henderson. Yes, Mrs. Doctor. I'll do your cleaning, call you 'ma'am', anything to get my son on that team.

She fingered her pearl-handled pocketknife. Maybe she didn't have a horse or wear feathers in her hair like a real Indian, but she had a real *knife*. Besides, she was the only girl on the rez to play knife-in-the-ground or *bechea-mapa-chewok*.

Mary Agnes knew how to position the knife on her forefinger. She knew just how to move her arm and flick her wrist, launching the knife into the circle drawn in the dirt. She figured she was still good with her knife; maybe later she'd practice her throws.

The March sun slanted through the open door of the Montana Bar. This was the only place Indians drank. All the other bars had window signs that read, "No Indians."

The barkeep stood behind the bar, smoking and squinting at the brightness. The air was chilly and street dusty, although, it didn't penetrate into the shadows or take away the stale air. Twelve bar stools with worn vinyl tops welcomed customers. Two booths, as well as two tables with mismatched chairs, completed the seating arrangements.

A man came out of the back room, carrying a case of Great Falls Select beer and stacked it in the bar fridge. He and the bartender talked about last night's fight when two Indian women had a heated discussion that ended on the sidewalk, including a lot of hair pulling, slapping and swearing before the sheriff's deputy hauled them both off to jail.

"Get you something, Mary Agnes?"

"Red beer." She fished coins from her fringed leather purse, then downed the mixture of tomato juice and beer and gestured for a refill. "My boy, Pretty Weasel, is trying out for the basketball team today."

"That so?" He lit another cig on the butt of the last one. "I didn't know you had a kid."

"He lives in Killdeer. I heard he shoots hoops all day, and can dribble like the Harlem Globetrotters. No one can steal the ball from him!"

"We could use some new talent on the team. Didn't even make the sectionals last year." He refilled her glass. "You going to watch?"

"Maybe." She took a long pull from her glass and licked the foam from the corner of her mouth. She was afraid that Pretty Weasel wouldn't want to see her.

⇶⋙⋘⋘

Mary Agnes perched on the church wall where she could view the gym door without being seen. She picked a dried lilac blossom and rolled one of the leaves into a pretend cig. The wait for Pretty Weasel gave her a chance to get off her feet. Cleaning white people's dirt tired her out. Her scuffed tennis shoes slipped to the ground.

High school basketball was important in these small Montana towns, a culture unto itself. Her grandma, Lillian Turns Plenty, had told her it'd replaced traditional Indian games. It was a way an Indian could shine. If Pretty Weasel made the team, maybe he wouldn't drop out of school like so many Indians before him. He might be so good even the white girls would date him.

Pressing closer to the lilac bush, she watched Pretty Weasel jump out of a pickup. She stared. Fine Boy, her pet name for him, had become a handsome young man with light tan skin, lean and sleek as a palomino.

She hadn't seen much of him as he grew up. Bonnie Sees Foxes, her cousin, had come for him. Mary Agnes, at fourteen, was unwed and too poor to support herself, let alone a child. Bonnie and her husband Carl were childless. In the Crow tradition, close relatives sometimes raised a child. Although it was the sensible thing to do, Mary Agnes never did forget the day when Bonnie took the warm, flannel-wrapped bundle from her arms.

Twenty minutes later, Coach Vernon and Pretty Weasel came out of the gym. Coach had the basketball tucked under his arm. Mary Agnes was dying to know how it went. She slipped into her shoes and crossed the street.

"Hi there," Mary Agnes said. Pretty Weasel didn't look at her. She wished she had a clean shirt on.

"What do you think, Coach?" Mary Agnes asked. "Isn't my boy a good player?"

"I may give him a try, although it's late in the season." Coach said. "He'll have to stay in school!"

Pretty Weasel nodded.

Coach slapped the ball to Pretty Weasel and walked to his car.

Mother and son stood in the parking lot. With a bitter jolt of his shoulder blades, he turned his back to her.

She put her hand on his arm. "You'll be handsome in your letter jacket."

He shrugged off her touch.

"I used to play basketball, too." She buried her hands in her jean pockets. "Can I tell you about it sometime?"

He was silent.

"Do you have a place to stay in town? My house is too far, I hitch to town."

"Drunks can't drive," Pretty Weasel said.

Mary Agnes looked at her shoes. She should have put the laces in. "I've had some bad luck."

Pretty Weasel turned to go.

"The reservation cops set me up."

"Yeah, sure." He walked away, the basketball tucked under his arm.

"Wait a sec," she called. "I'll ask Mrs. Henderson, the doctor's wife, about housing. I work for her."

"I'll find my own place."

"I can help a little with the rent," she said to his back. "I've got something special I've been saving for you."

Chapter Three

Patsy Olsen had three heads under the cone-shaped hair dryers that resembled a row of silver Atlas missiles ready to fire. Another head in the sink and one more stuck in a magazine. That was the way she liked it—wash, set, comb out, spray with extra-hold and collect! Only open a week, she desperately needed cash to secure her bank loan.

Patsy sipped her third cup of coffee as she surveyed her small kingdom. It was only a ten-by-thirty foot trailer, set behind the high school just off Highway Two in Bowman, Montana. She was proud of it, and felt so grateful to her friend, Ed, who'd co-signed for her loan.

All the current magazines—*Silver Screen, Life, Look* and *The Ladies Home Journal*—rested on her table. She had two turquoise sinks, a matching toilet in a small cubicle and pink organdy curtains. On the floor were fluffy pink rugs and pink lace curtains covered the windows. Patsy hoped the town ladies wouldn't be able to resist her skillful fingers and feminine salon.

"Hello? I'm about to cook under here." Helen lifted her dryer hood and dabbed at her apple-cheeks.

"Hold your water," Patsy told her. "I'll get to you in a sec. You can pull out the bobby pins."

Patsy evaluated her next customer, Mrs. Vernon. She was commonplace in features, average height and weight, and just a little dowdy in her nylon blouse with a bow at the neck. Her power lay in her pure, peaches-and-cream complexion. What could she do to pick up Mrs. Vernon's appearance, get her to prize herself a little more?

"Mrs. Vernon, good to meet you. With your nice thick hair, you might consider a new do. Something poufy, not done with pin curls." She gestured to the reflection in the mirror.

"Let's pull your hair away from your face." Patsy waved her comb like a baton at a concert. "Your skin, by the way, is flawless! Do you bathe in milk, for God's sake?" Patsy touched Lois's cheek. "You just need a more up-to-date style."

"I don't know—I've been wearing my hair like this for years." Lois Vernon pushed her cinnamon-colored hair behind her pink, shell-like ears. "You think I could look younger?"

"We'll get rid of the Mamie Eisenhower bangs. Look at this style." Patsy handed her the September issue of *Silver Screen* with Liz Taylor on the cover. "I could deepen your color, give you some height on the top and spit curls on the side."

"Why would I want to look like her? She stole Eddie Fisher from Debbie Reynolds." She turned her head from the mirror. "Deepen the color? You mean dye?" She lowered her voice and said, "I'm not that kind."

"Wouldn't Mr. Vernon like you getting fixy?" Patsy asked.

"You know my husband?"

"I see him arrive for school every morning with a kid. Your daughter?"

"Bobbi's fourteen. I hardly know what to do with her anymore. She's a handful!"

"Fourteen was a hard time in *my* life." Patsy thought of the heavy responsibilities she'd had as a teen.

"Bring your daughter in sometime, and I'll give her a haircut. About your hubby, can I call him Coach?"

"Sure, everyone does."

"Well, he's a real looker. You've gotta keep up."

"I swear he never really notices me any more. We've been married forever. Do you know what that's like?"

"I'm pretty qualified on the subject of marriage. Two times. One more and I'm out!" Patsy said. With a twinge of regret, she recalled her early marriage to Ronnie, and later to Ord, who'd been her one true love.

Mrs. Vernon patted the back of her hair. "Mag, my best friend, thinks I need a new style, too. Believe I'll try the rollers."

Best friend. Patsy pictured Sheri's bruised face and black eye. Where was her friend now? There was just nothing more she could do for Sheri. She needed to focus on building her own business.

"What about the color?" Patsy asked. "Get you real stylish for the weekend, Mrs. Vernon?"

"Not today for the tint, just the set for the weekend. Saturday, we have the first steak fry of the year. Mag Henderson is wearing a white strapless sundress embroidered with red cherries, red pumps, and," she covered her mouth and whispered, "a long line bra."

Patsy smoothed the back of Lois's styling gown. "You have a nice full figure. What are you wearing?"

Mrs. Henderson barged in the door, a cloud of perfume and cigarette smoke whirling around her head. She was a leggy blonde, her dark red lipstick framing a smile as large as Texas.

"Am I late?" She gave everybody a wave. "I was instructing my cleaning lady. She didn't know how to fold the contour sheets. She wants me to do something for her son. Apparently, he wants to play ball at the high school."

Patsy took a check from a customer, grimaced at the lack of tip and snapped it in her cash drawer. "Take a seat, please. I'll get you a glass of water."

"Anything stronger?" Mrs. Henderson asked. "And call me Mag."

"Don't we wish," Patsy filled two glasses at the shampoo sink. A little drinkie would be good right now. She handed one to her client and took long pulls from her own. The Dramamine she'd been taking at night left her tongue sticking to her teeth. She couldn't sleep without it, too worried about her finances and the late night phone calls.

"Hello, hello," she'd say. No one would answer.

Mrs. Henderson plopped herself in the swivel chair for her wash and set. Patsy lifted the back of her hair. "This shade you're using is a little off. Too brassy."

"I have a great gal in Great Falls that does my color."

Patsy frowned. "You don't need to leave town, Mag, I'd love to do your color this time. Look at my hair, shiny and honey blonde straight from the bottle."

"Hmm, I don't know," Mag glanced at Lois, "What do you think?"

Patsy put her hands on her hips, "Tell ya what, if you don't like it, I'll refund your dough." Shittoosie, she thought, I can't afford to do that. However, the memory of the guy at the bank as he stared at her legs, implying other arrangements could be made, spurred her on. "Yup, a full refund! And here's the color chart with swatches of real hair." It was worth a try, as the doctor's wife, Mag had some clout.

As Mag studied the samples, Patsy did a comb-out on Helen. She sprayed with a practiced flourish, and then passed Helen the mirror to view the back.

"Is it supposed to stick out on the sides like that?"

"Yes, that's the new look. It should hold until next week, and don't forget to check the back every morning. Don't you see ladies that have a flat spot on the back where they slept?"

Helen frowned. "Well, I can't sleep sitting up, so I use a hairnet."

"A hairnet? That's no good." Patsy pointed to her own hair teased to a shiny blonde helmet. "Five days now and four nights on this do. The secret—want to hear the really big secret?" All the ladies in the shop listened up. "I wrap my head in toilet paper."

"Toilet paper?" Helen asked. "That's quite wasteful, isn't it? TP costs a lot, especially the two-ply. It would come out of my kitchen money."

Patsy laughed. "I wrap my head at night. When I get up, I blow my nose on the toilet paper and then use it for my morning pee. No waste there."

Mag hooted.

"So Mag, what do you think about the Champagne Blonde? Good with your beige complexion." She swiveled her hips. "Blondes have more fun!"

"Can you make it that exact hue?"

"Easier than changing your nail polish."

"I'll give it a try. Especially," she winked at Lois, "with the money-back guarantee. There is one big problem going so light . . ."

"What?"

Mag lifted her skirt and exposed her peach satin panties. Instantly, she had everyone's attention. Red faces popped out from under the dryers. The head came out from behind the magazine.

"I won't match." Mag pointed. "Down there!"

The heads giggled, then guffawed, then laughter swirled around the trailer, ruffled the curtains, and curled the throw rugs. Finally, the storm was over, and two ladies rushed to the bathroom claiming they'd wet their panties. Then someone muttered, *down there,* and the laughter circled for another round.

Chapter Four

B obbi met Pretty Weasel the next week.

"Can I go?" she begged when Mag's Cadillac roared into the driveway with a sharp beep of the horn for Bobbi's mother, Lois.

"To the reservation?" Mag raised one plucked eyebrow as Lois got in the car. "We're just going to drop off these old coats, and maybe see a ball player."

Bobbi stood by the car and hunched her shoulders. "Marlene got to go for Cokes with her friends."

Lois looked at Mag, who claimed she knew everything about raising children.

"Okay, Kiddo." Mag called Bobbi, her sister Marlene, and even her own five kids, Kiddo, as if they were just so many marbles in a bag.

"Jump in. We're going to cast an eye on Donny Pretty Weasel, a ball player. As a favor to my cleaning lady, his mother, Mary Agnes." She winked at Lois. "He could be a real cutie."

The women were decked out like it was bridge club day. Lois wore her blue-flowered sundress with spaghetti straps that showed a fair amount of skin. Freshly ironed, the dress smelled of starch. Mag had squeezed into red capris, a white blouse, and a hot pink neck scarf, with her mink tossed over her shoulders.

"Jeez, Louise." Bobbi plugged her nose as she piled in the back seat. "Do you have to wear an ocean of perfume?" She kicked the back of Lois's seat. "Why do you guys do everything together? That's so geeky—even your ironing!" She kicked the seat again. "And why do you have to doll up all the time?"

Lois swatted Bobbi's legs. "You could spiff up a little."

"I rolled up my jeans."

At Nashua they barreled onto a gravel road. Mag smoked with one hand and steered with the Necker knob. Gravel smacked the bottom of the car like buckshot, and a cloud of dust rolled behind them.

Bobbi slumped in the back with her eyes closed. Playing possum so she could spy on the grownups. Lois eyed Bobbi and lowered her voice.

"I feel silly dressed up like this, Mag." She tugged her skirt over her knees. "We're rushing the season with our summer outfits."

"My winter clothes are so tired!" Mag swerved to miss a cow ambling across the road and the car slid in the gravel.

"Why are we dressing up for the Indian reservation?" Lois asked.

"To look pretty! We'll stop on the way home at the Elks Club for a drink. That'll make Coach jealous. The worst thing you can do for a man's attention is sit around and wait for it."

"He expects me to be home to fix supper."

"Just a quick cocktail. Then over dessert you can tell him if Pretty Weasel's as good as they say. Let Coach see you in a new role—a pretty woman and helper."

"Does Robert mind if you're out and about?"

"He's so busy delivering babies, he doesn't care what I do."

"Coach, I don't know—he never talks to me about the players. Or the team."

Mag tapped her red fingernail on her teeth. "That can change."

"He's worried about his job. Without a good season, they could can him. The team needs some wins, and that's all he ever thinks about. He doesn't even pay attention to the girls." She pulled down the visor and checked her lipstick. "I'm sick of it!"

Mag glanced back at Bobbi and whispered, "Have you noticed Duffy? He's been checking you out? Coach should catch that drift!"

"The assistant coach? He's married with four kids."

"What does that matter? Men still look."

"Coach didn't notice my new do."

"Bet he would eyeball blondie, the beautician!" She touched the back of her hair. "Patsy knows her stuff, and I love my new color. What do you think about inviting her to the steak fry?"

"A *hairdresser*?" Lois tugged on the front of her dress. "Is this too low?"

"Jeez, no, you have great tits. I bet you still have pink nipples."

Lois glanced back at Bobbi and held her finger to her lips.

Nipples came in different colors? Bobbi wanted to hear more. And problems with her parents—her mom felt bad 'cause dad ignored her? This was scary news. Dad *was* away from home a lot with teaching, coaching, hunting and fishing. Was that why the headboard action had vanished?

"How 'bout if I line up Patsy with the new band teacher, just so we have our eye on her? Keep the kitties off the street!"

"Good call."

The thirty miles to the reservation took some time. Bored with the strip-farmed wheat fields—black and yellow, black and yellow, Bobbi fell asleep.

They finally screeched up to the Quonset hut. Lois fluffed her hair, and then peered in her compact at her already red lips. Bobbi re-rolled her jeans.

Over the front door was a hand-painted sign, "Welcome, Freda Beasley."

Bobbi nudged her mom. "Who's that?"

Mag rolled her eyes. "Some Indian woman. I heard she's a troublemaker."

Bobbi resolved to find out more. She liked troublemakers.

They entered a large room that reeked of sweat, beer, and dust. With basketball hoops at each end, table and chairs on the sides, it looked like a combination of Bingo hall and basketball court.

A stocky woman ambled over. "Ladies?"

"Hello." Mag used her lady-of-the-manor voice. "Do you know Mary Agnes Lone Hill? We came to see her boy, Pretty Weasel, as a favor."

"He'll be here any minute for practice. I'm Dede Blue Beads." Dede, in denim coveralls, stood with her legs apart and her chin stuck out like she knew things they didn't. Important things.

"We brought coats," Lois volunteered.

"A little late in the season."

"They'll be good next year, too." Mag tore open a pack of Pall Malls. She stuck one in her mouth and handed another to Dede like it was a gold nugget.

"So who's Freda Beasley?" Bobbi asked.

Dede pulled on her cig. "Like you're interested in an Indian woman."

Just then a guy bounded from the shadows, dribbling a basketball—first in tight circles, then behind his back, then hand to hand. Under the basket he twirled 360° in the air and dunked the ball. He grabbed the rebound in one hand and brought it to his other hand with a resounding slap.

Pretty Weasel's skin was light for an Indian—his glistening black hair, crisp as lettuce, was swept back in a ducktail. He was tall, at

BARBARA MEYER LINK

least six feet, and graceful as an antelope—a beautiful blur of arms and legs. Clearly he was no ordinary ballplayer, no ordinary Indian!

No one could look away. Their heads followed each flowing motion back and forth as if on a string. Mag was speechless, and Lois stunned.

"Hey, Mrs. Vernon, are you scouting me, too? Coach thinks I'm okay." He slapped the ball into her hands.

"Hi, you must be Donny. This is my daughter, Roberta, I mean Bobbi. Bobbi with an 'i.'" She couldn't stop staring at him. Finally, she pushed the ball back.

"Mrs. Coach and Mrs. Doctor come a-calling." He nodded at Bobbi. "Want to shoot a few Bobbi with an 'i'?"

"Uh—" Bobbi wanted to disappear. She watched him dribble and shoot, dribble and shoot, putting on a show. And what a show! Her Mom waved a manicured hand in her face like she needed to cool off, Mag let out a soft whistle, and Dede clapped. Bobbi was paralyzed until Mag shoved her. Then, with her jeans flapping on her thin legs, she raced after him.

He shot from all over the court and bounced the ball to Bobbi. "Your turn, kid."

With all her might she tossed the ball. It arced like a pop fly, and plunged three feet short of the basket.

"Puny! Your Dad's the coach? Didn't he teach you anything? Here, stand with your toes just behind the free throw line, hold the ball between your legs, bend your knees and use your body." He demonstrated, and the ball floated through the strings.

Yeah, she thought, why didn't my Dad teach me? Girls can play, too! Then, she followed instructions and the ball clunked off the rim.

"That's better."

She tried again and missed.

"One more time."

Bobbi eyed the basket. It looked as far away as the moon; no way she would make it. She turned to her mom. "Isn't it time to go? I have homework to do or washing dishes or something."

"Shoot," Pretty Weasel ordered. "You're plenty tall enough." He put the ball in her hands.

Mag chuckled.

Bobbi bent her knees slowly all the way down and all the way up and launched her shot. The ball swished through the net. A clean shot.

He whistled. "Indians are good for *something*, aren't they?"

"I can toss chokecherries up and catch them in my mouth. Except once, I got some stuck in my throat. I ran around the house, choking and flapping. Like this . . ." Bobbi waved her arms like a giant bird. Now what made her do that? She could feel her ears burning.

"Well, Chokecherry Girl, practice hard. Catch you later, ladies; you can find me in the Montana. Oh, and make sure you give Coach a good report." He loped away, knowing all eyes were on him. Mag turned to Lois with a triumphant smile and mouthed *wow*!

And cloud nine for Bobbi. Pretty Weasel liked her! He taught her to shoot, and gave her an Indian name. She could write a term paper, thirty pages at least, on his tawny skin, his brows like crow's wings, his kissable lips, and his white shorts low on his hips playing chicken with gravity. Wait 'til she laid it out to Rita and Donna.

Holy Mary, Mother of teen-age Jesus, Bobbi thought, I'm in love!

Pretty Weasel returned to the gym after his admiring audience of Bobbi, Mag and Lois had gone. He and Dede sat and had a smoke.

"You impressed 'em, kid. Been practicing?"

He ran a comb through his hair. "Every day! Think I'm good enough to make Bowman's team?"

"I do. Remember, Coach has a reputation for being hard on Indian players. It wouldn't hurt for his wife and daughter to add a good word."

"Do *you* think I'm good enough?"

"Are you kidding me? The girls' team I played on was better than Bowman's varsity now."

"You played?" he asked.

"Ages ago, junior high and high school. We won the regionals one year. It was a close game, and in the end it was decided by a free throw."

Pretty Weasel grabbed the basketball, stood at the free-throw line and swished one in. Then he seized the rebound and quickly sank five more.

He looked smug. "I shoot a hundred in practice."

"How many do you make?" Dede asked.

"At the rez, even on our crummy backboards with the crooked rims, I've sunk eighty-nine."

"Damn!" Dede's jowls shook. "It runs in the family!"

"How so?" Pretty Weasel asked.

She snapped the rubber band on her braid. "Maybe you don't want to hear this—your real mother, Mary Agnes Lone Hill, was a hell of a ball player!"

Pretty Weasel's face closed like a slammed door. "I got nothing from Lone Hill. She gave me away when I was three months old, and I never saw her again."

"There was a lot of pressure from her clan and, for God's sake, she was even too poor to buy milk for you. And Bonnie and Carl were crazy to get a child."

"So you say." Pretty Weasel turned away.

The clock in the gym ticked—minutes passed in silence.

Dede's face hardened. "Kid, and you *are* a kid! She was torn from her family and sent to an Indian School, only *fourteen* when you were born!"

"How'd she get pregnant anyway? Was she a slut?"

"Listen to me!" Dede slapped her hips. "I wasn't always this size, you know. I was on her team, and I'll tell you how it went down. Then *you* decide if she never gave you anything!"

He folded his arms across his chest. "Bonnie is my mother. Nothing you say is going to change *my* mind."

"Hear me out. Years ago people were just as basketball crazy as they are now. Our junior high team was in the championship round. The whole town turned out for our game, and the gym was full to the rafters. The cheering and yelling, even at the beginning of the game, was deafening. The old Indian women pounded their canes and the men gave war whoops. Mary Agnes didn't play in the first quarter as the coach was saving her for later. She could rack up points, but often fouled out."

Pretty Weasel drummed his fingers on the table. "Sloppy playing."

Dede continued. "We held our own against Plentywood, and only fell behind at the end of the first half. Mary Agnes started in the second half. We gave her good feeds, and she scored three baskets. Then their defense picked her up and froze her out. Plentywood missed a few shots, and we pulled five points ahead. Coach called a time out, told us to use a full-court press."

Pretty Weasel nodded. "Man to man? Or zone?"

Dede chuckled. "Girl to girl. We kept them away from their basket. Eventually, they broke through, and we ended up in overtime. Everyone was up and stomping, and the gym was shaking."

"I love it when the crowd gets into it!" Pretty Weasel jumped up and dribbled twice around the table.

Dede nodded. "The overtime stayed even. After a free throw, they pulled ahead by one. Mary Agnes got the ball and raced to the basket. As she started to shoot she got an elbow to her ribs and went down—the wind knocked out of her."

Pretty Weasel rubbed his chest with his fist.

"Luckily, she was okay and had two shots—one to tie and the second for the win. I saw her look up in the stands where her Aunt Judy used to sit and wave her medicine feather."

"Did she make 'em?" Pretty Weasel was gripping his basketball, as if he wanted to shoot. "That's a lot of pressure."

"Her first shot was clean. She bounced the ball twice and went up for the second. Instantly, the Bowman scoreboard flashed the winning score, and we pounded her back yelling '*Mary, Mary, Mary!*'" Dede passed her hand over her face as if *she* were exhausted from playing. "It was something to see!"

"I bet," Pretty Weasel agreed. "I know what it's like—the noise, the heat, the sweat in your eyes, the feeling when you make a perfect shot." His face looked alive, like he'd just gotten some good news. "Yeah, I know *that* feeling."

"After the game we rode around with Larry Star Boy, all five of us piled in the back seat. As he cruised Front Street, we yelled and waved pompoms. Your mom hugged us all and cried. *She was a hero that night!*

Dede leaned into his face. Her words rolled out with spit. "So don't say *she* never gave you nothing. She got you into a good home and passed on her *love* of basketball *and* her talent!"

Later, Pretty Weasel sipped his soda. He'd gone through the drive-up window at the Hi Hat after talking with Dede. Should he press his case with the coach's wife? Turning up the radio, he drummed his hands on the steering wheel. In time with Fats Domino.

And what about Coach's daughter? She was sure to give him a good review. Plucky kid. He'd pushed her until she made a basket.

And her mom, Coach's pretty wife, Lois, he'd look for her at the Montana. Her friend Mag was a pistol, they'd show. He'd have another chance to pitch his cause.

As for his so-called *real* mother, Mary Agnes, he felt embarrassed by the stories of her drinking and her shack by the river. He remembered getting a package from her when he was ten—a small plastic truck, like he was still a little boy. Some mother. Maybe she'd had a hard time at the Indian school and as a teen mom. What was that to him now?

He tossed his empty Coke cup out the window.

Chapter Five

The same week Bobbi met Pretty Weasel, she made an important discovery about her mom. She lived for spying on the grown-ups. In fact, yesterday after school, she'd been lurking around the beauty shop trailer. There was something weird about the blonde floozy staring at her dad.

Bobbi had been secretly driving for a year. Pretty much taught herself in their Nash Rambler, although sometimes she'd take the station wagon. Her dad kept both cars in back with the keys in the ignition, and no one noticed when Bobbi used a car. Her sister, Marlene, didn't drive; she thought it was uncool for girls. Wheels, for Bobbi, were everything!

Her mom didn't drive, either. Not after she got drunk at Mag's and creamed their wood-paneled station wagon four months ago. How had she missed the wide-as-North-Dakota driveway? The ensuing fight between her parents was fierce. The words "drunken sluts," broke the ice, meaning mom and Mag. Then her mom yelled that he was a terrible father—away from home all the time, a bad coach, and that he would never have a winning team. Then her dad screamed more swear words, terrible words Bobbi had never heard before. The rest of the fight was more of the same, except it ended with her mom throwing her shoes. Was this normal for parents to fight like this? She'd put her pillow over her head to block them out.

However, after the crash, her mom never lacked for rides. She seemed to have miracle powers over people with cars. Got them to cart her around like she was some kind of invalid. Like she'd just gotten out of an iron lung.

The night of Bobbi's discovery, she'd lurked on the front lawn until Mag's car pulled into the driveway. Earlier after a phone call, her Mom mentioned going out. Were they accepting Pretty Weasel's invite to the Montana Bar? Bobbi stationed herself in the shadows so she could watch Mag's car as it pulled up in the driveway.

"Ready?" Mag's whisper was louder than most cheerleaders with a megaphone. "He might be there tonight. Hurry up!"

"Are you sure this is a good idea?" Lois whispered as she stood by the car. "It makes me nervous going out at night."

"Where's Coach?" Mag asked.

"Reffing a game in Culbertson. Back after midnight."

What was up? Bobbi was more than curious and slipped into the station wagon to follow them, coasting down the hill without lights and then popping the clutch to start the car. They turned on Second Avenue. Parking at the Elks Club, they sidled around the corner and into the Montana Bar.

Bobbi parked across the street, too scared to swallow her own spit. In the first place married women only went out alone at night to baby showers and Tupperware parties. They didn't go to bars, and only Indians drank at the Montana, which had a reputation for serving under age drinkers.

Is this what Mag meant by a little excitement? She knew Mag liked to party. Bobbi had seen her take a slug from a silver flask at bridge club. Why not drink at a regular place like the Elks Club? Were they meeting up with Pretty Weasel? No, it couldn't be him.

Maybe it was the assistant coach, Duffy, who flirted with all the women. In any case, *it was not cool!* She pressed her forehead on the steering wheel.

Once, late at night while coming home from babysitting, she'd seen two Indian women fighting on bar street. They'd pulled hair and ripped each other's shirts. She'd spotted a dirty bra strap and a saggy brown breast, and felt sick, like the time she'd eaten a giant bowl of radishes with salt. Like how she felt now.

What on earth was going on with her parents? First the big fight when mom wrecked the car. Then January and February with no headboard banging, then the weird trip to the reservation to see an Indian ball player, then the floozy at the beauty shop watching her dad. Now, her mom was going into an Indian bar at night.

Oh hell and Jesus help her, couldn't they just act like parents?

Bobbi stared at the bar until her eyes about crossed. They never came out, at least not through the front door. On her way home she cruised through her neighborhood, glancing in lighted windows. She saw a mom drying dishes, a couple of kids eating popcorn and playing cards. She wished she had some of dad's popcorn. He fixed it on the stove, shaking the pan to keep it from burning. It was the best popcorn she ever ate.

All of a sudden, she surprised herself with big, gulping sobs. She didn't know if it was about her mom going in a bar at night or that woman staring at her dad or the dead baby. Whatever it was, she put her face in her hands and cried.

Chapter Six

Bobbi slouched in English class on the Monday morning after she'd met Pretty Weasel. She never thought an Indian boy could be so cute, and she'd spent the weekend in a haze imagining all kinds of things. Just thinking about him made her panties wet, and she squirmed in her desk.

First, he would call. No, better yet, she'd slip into practice waiting for her dad. Pretty Weasel would walk her to Dad's car and ask her out for a Coke. Next a movie, followed by a sock-hop, and then they'd be a couple. She could picture herself wearing his letter jacket. The jacket would be impossibly baggy and the leather sleeves would cover her hands making her look little and cute. She'd wear the jacket open to display his class ring on a chain. And when he made the winning baskets everyone would hug her. And when they lost a game, everyone would look at her to see how she was taking the loss.

She barely heard the new teacher call roll. "Roberta Vernon." When the class snickered, she blushed. *Ro-ber-ta, for God's sake*, too many syllables.

"Here," she raised one finger like a weary movie star. "It's Bobbi."

She traced the worn initials carved on the desk, R. J., circled by an ink heart. The ragged window shade flapped in the morning breeze. Maybe she wanted to be a woman wrestler or a cocktail waitress. No way was she going to be a housewife like her mother, crocheting tea towels and washing china.

Bobbi watched Miss Bauer, the most interesting thing since Mr. Wainwright, the science teacher, had a heart attack and died in the boiler room. She stalked back and forth in front of the class. *Holden Caulfield,* she wrote on the blackboard, her fingernails bitten to the quick.

"Alienation," she said. "That's your assignment. Look for that theme in the reading."

Bobbi took her time picking up her books. Donna and Rita crowded the teacher's desk—their faces like the wise men at the manger. However, the new teacher extended her hand to Bobbi. "I'm Miss Bauer. I saw you gawking at my car."

Bobbi shook her hand. Dry as summer sand with a grip like a logger.

"Are you from California?" Bobbi asked.

"I taught there briefly." Miss Bauer picked at a callus on her palm. "I ended up here. I'd like to take a look around—maybe a tour. Any ideas?"

When Bobbi suggested she drive to Fort Peck Lake, she invited the girls to come along. Rita and Donna nodded. Then, Bobbi nodded. They looked like puppets. Their heads bobbing up and down, up and down—already under her spell.

Miss Bauer straightened out the curves on the Fort Peck Highway. The wind whipped their hair like it'd been bad. Bobbi entered a new world—speed, cold wind with laughing, flying words. She wanted the magical ride to last forever.

"Call me Jean when we're out of school," Miss Bauer said, hiking her skirt up to straddle the bench in the picnic area.

Bobbi thought the silver lake and the trees, their branches reaching for the sky, had never looked so pretty. Jean passed out Pall Malls. They cupped their hands and lit up. Bobbi didn't dare inhale, so as not to spoil the moment with coughing. After all, they could be movie stars in cocktail lounges with the smoke circling their heads like perfume. Even the shivering aspen leaves seem to twinkle just for them.

"Look here." Jean brought out a package of cookies. "I bet you like Oreos. Let's see who can build the highest stack of fillings."

They carefully peeled discs of sugary white from each one and stacked the fillings between two cookie halves. Bobbi built a giant tower of eleven fillings that collapsed when she took a bite. Frosting and cookie bits flew everywhere. Rita got twelve fillings and Jean got fifteen. Fallen bits, they decided, were to be picked up with their tongues. So there they were, tongues to the table like cats lapping spilled milk, cigs in their hands, giggling like fools. In a lull, Rita poked Bobbi in the ribs, and they started hooting all over again.

Bobbi tried inhaling and got so dizzy she had to lie on the bare ground. Donna and Rita joined her. "Look," she said grabbing their hands and gyrating her arms and legs while looking into the cloudless sky. "We're bopping. We're sky bopping."

Jean sat beside them. "You girls are so much fun. I've missed being around kids."

Fun? They were lowly freshmen. No one wanted to be with them. Was she on the teen planet or the adult planet?

Jean slid toward Bobbi. "You're the ticklish one?"

She glared at Rita. "Sort of."

Rita hooted. "Her sister tickles her until she wets her pants."

"Really?" Jean looked interested. "I can help you with that. I used to be ticklish, too." She lightly ran her hand over Bobbi's ribs until she jerked away.

Bobbi was late getting home, and they who must be obeyed waited. She sneaked in the kitchen door, hoping everyone had died or at least been taken to the hospital. The supper dishes were piled high in the drainer and draped with a towel like over a fat corpse. Her dad stood in the living room, his back to Bobbi.

She tried to sprint past him.

"Just a minute, young lady."

"Sorry, Dad." She slowly backed away. "I got delayed. Big school project."

"Bobbi?" He tamped on his pipe and took his time lighting it. "I called the school. Where *were* you?"

"Ya, well, you know the new teacher—Miss Bauer? She had never been to Fort Peck or seen the dam." She balanced on one leg. "We kind of went with her on a drive."

"A tour? With a teacher?" He moved the pipe to the other side of his mouth. "The new teacher? Lois, come here." Could he smell the cigarette smoke on her? Bobbi felt guilty. Like she had done more than smoke and get home late.

"*You* can wait in your room."

Bobbi strolled to her room as if she didn't care. Really, that car ride felt so worth it—the wind, the smell of the leather, the silver-rushing highway. She peered in the mirror over her desk. Different. All at once, her eyebrows resembled Audrey Hepburn's.

Bobbi would give her *Silver Screen* collection for a cig right now. Wouldn't that be a gas if they caught her puffing out her window? She stuck her ear to the door.

"Lois, for God's sake, where *are* you?" Her mom usually came running when he called her. "Gossip, unnatural, the school board," she heard him say. She scrambled away from her door when they appeared in her doorway.

"Roberta, you're grounded for the weekend. And," he said as he gave her shoulder a shake, "you are not to go *anywhere* with that teacher. In fact, I think you need a job."

Patsy was taking out the garbage when she noticed Coach walking over from the school. Her knees and elbows felt like Jell-O. Why hadn't she washed her hair? At least she'd worn a cute pink smock, and had brushed her teeth after lunch.

He held out his hand and introduced himself.

"I'm Patsy Olson. I see you arriving at school with your daughter."

Coach nodded.

"Nice that you can take her to school."

He ran his hand over his chin. His four o'clock shadow had kicked in early.

"It helps me keep an eye on her. Her older sister Marlene is no problem, studies hard and makes no trouble. Bobbi's another story!"

Patsy wondered what this had to do with her. However, it felt worth it just to see him up close. He was a compact man with dark brown eyes and a distracted look. His weight flowed from his legs to his torso to his arms to a full strong neck. There was a drag to his shoulders that made her sad, reminding her of her ex-husband Ord and how he'd looked the last time she saw him.

"Are you worried about Bobbi?" she asked.

"Some. Her mother can't handle her, and I don't have the time. Really, I shouldn't bother you with this."

"It's okay. How old is she?"

"Fourteen. Do you have any kids?"

She felt a pain she didn't know she still had. "No." She chewed a hangnail. "Could have, except things went wrong for me." She felt exposed and confused. Why was she confiding in a stranger, when she hadn't thought about her lost baby for years? She could have been the mother of a teen by now.

Coach looked at his watch. "I've got practice. Here's what I had in mind. By the number of cars here, you look pretty busy. I wondered if you could use a helper? Bobbi would do a good job—she has a lot of energy if directed. Could she do a couple hours after school and Saturdays? I think it'd keep her busy and away from a bad situation."

Yes, she needed the help; although, she couldn't afford much. How could she turn down those gorgeous eyes? What kind of trouble was Bobbi flirting with? Could only be boys. Was this an opportunity to head off a disastrous teen pregnancy like she'd had?

"Tell you what. I can't afford much, just starting out here. Let's go for two hours after school and three on Saturday."

His smile transformed his face. "Thanks!" As he walked away, his shoulders looked relaxed and his step was bouncy.

Patsy folded her arms across her chest. Wrapped up in her own worries, she'd forgotten it took so little to make someone else happy.

Now she looked forward to meeting the third member of the Vernon family, the incorrigible Bobbi. Whatever was happening in the Vernon family—a neglected wife, a troubled teen. It couldn't be worse than Patsy's own childhood.

Chapter Seven

1935

Almost every evening during the summer of 1935, it was pretty much the same routine. The three little girls waited in the back seat of the Ford while their parents drank at the Stockman's Bar and listened to the ballgame.

Around seven Audrey and Buzzy would arrive home from the cafe where they worked, waiting tables and cooking.

"Hi, babies." Audrey would aim some pats in their direction like she was happy to see them. "Let's load up." Already in their pajamas, thanks to Patsy, the girls crawled in the back seat, each carrying her things in a pillowcase.

"Brought you some burgers," Audrey said. "And a piece of rhubarb pie to share." She passed a greasy paper sack to the back seat. They drove the few blocks and parked on the street where all the bars were in Malta, Montana.

"Just going in for a couple of beers and the game. Might be another pennant for the Yankees! Come in and get us if you need anything." Audrey waved; she was the real baseball fan and Buzzy liked a lot of cold ones.

In the dusty cave of the back seat, the girls looked abandoned. Patsy had just turned seven, Carole was six, and Sharon was four.

"Where's Sally?" Patsy had asked at the beginning of summer.

"Buzzy can't pay Sally to babysit this summer. You're seven—you can watch your sisters." She pulled up the strap on Sharon's pinafore. "Buzzy said we need the money for milk and rent."

"Sally taught us to play slapjack." Patsy said. "Once she bought us root beer."

"You'll be just fine in the car. Patsy, you're in charge now."

Patsy pulled a kitchen knife and plastic plates from her bag. She cut the burgers in quarters, "Don't spill, you know Buzzy hates spots." For some unknown reason, the girls called their parents by their first names instead of Mom and Dad.

The girls cleared a place on the seat for their nightly game of slapjack. Patsy pulled the worn blue and white Bicycle cards from her pillowcase—some were creased, some were missing a corner. She carefully turned them over one by one. When a jack showed up, they each tried to be the first to slap it. All the cards underneath belonged to the first slapper; the one with the most cards won. Sharon mistakenly hit a queen and scattered the cards all over the floor.

"Let's start again. I'll shuffle." Patsy said.

They hit harder and harder, sometimes with both hands. Then they'd bang the hand of the person who had slapped first.

Sharon licked her small, chubby fingers. "It hurts."

"Mine, too." Carole rummaged in her pillowcase. "Let's play dolls."

Patsy understood this game. From tending to her sisters, she knew all about the drudgery of feeding and changing. She'd brought her doll, small dishes, spoons and tiny bottles, as did her sisters.

Patsy was a no-nonsense mother and put her doll down for the night after her bottle. Sometimes, Patsy's favorite red-haired doll did naughty things like kick off her blankets and she'd spank her. Something she often felt like doing to her younger sisters, but never did.

When the sun-red sky faded into dark blue, Patsy led the girls through the alley to the back of the bar. They slipped in the door to the small, dirty ladies' bathroom to brush their teeth and pee. Back in the car, they got ready to bed down.

"Oh, oh, duck," Patsy said. "Here comes Meckler."

Carole and Sharon dove to the floor as Patsy locked the doors.

Meckler was Malta's crazy—a World War 1 veteran. In knee-high boots, he strode around town—like he had a wind at his back. Newspapers and a scythe protruded from his ever-present cloth bag. Muttering under his breath, he was feared, although it was not certain he had hurt or even threatened anyone.

Tonight, Meckler did something new. He came over to the car and stood by the window. The girls stayed down, their faces pressed into the floorboards. They held their breath. Patsy softly counted as far as she could. At one hundred and fifty-seven, she cautiously raised her head. "He's gone."

They squirmed into sleeping positions. Carole twisted her hair as she drifted off, Sharon slipped her thumb in her mouth, and Patsy wished, as she did every night, that she was home in her own bed with her Dad, washing up after a pancake supper while her Mom smoked on the porch.

It was a July evening three years later. The setting sun, like an open fan, spread long rays of orange and red across the sky. The temperature had hit one hundred and two, by no means a record, and the sun took its time to descend. The streets were empty, no one going anywhere.

Again, the Ford was parked in front of the bar, Audrey and Buzzy were inside. In the hot backseat, the sisters leaned on each other like half-empty sacks of flour.

"No slapjack tonight. I'm suffocating," Patsy said. "We're going into the bar. I don't care if I get a spanking!"

Patsy paused in the doorway, the girls beside her. She always wondered what it was like inside. From the car she could see the red and green neon Budweiser sign. It cheerfully blinked off and on, reminding her of Christmas.

The drinkers stared at the girls in their seersucker pinafores and braids. "Whose brats?" someone muttered.

"Girls, girls," Audrey said as they headed for her table. "Can't you wait in the car? We'll be out in a few minutes."

Patsy planted herself on a chair. "We're afraid of Meckler. He stands by the car."

"You can stay for a few minutes."

Everyone resumed drinking and ignored the girls except Buzzy. He brought them Cokes. They sucked the sweet, dark liquid and clinked the ice in their glasses.

Buzzy and Audrey drifted back to the bar. Patsy looked around the room. It wasn't what she had imagined. Nobody danced or seemed to have much fun. The patrons leaned on the bar and pushed their cans of beer around. The floor looked real dirty, and her chair wobbled. She scratched the mosquito bite on her ankle until she felt warm sticky blood.

"When can we go home?" Carole asked, kicking the chair legs. Then she kicked Sharon, who started to cry. "I want to lie down."

"You can't. I want to go home, too, you little brats!" Patsy said. "Here, you can share the rest of my Coke."

They crunched the ice and licked cool drops from their straws.

"I wish I'd brought the cards," Patsy said. "We could play slapjack in here."

"Cards? You girls play cards?" The man at the next table apparently overheard.

"Hi," he said and held out his hand. "I'm Jared."

Patsy shook. It was like thrusting her hand into a burlap bag.

"I'm Patsy," she said. "I'm eleven. These are my sisters, Carole and Sharon."

"No, you're not," Carole said. "You're only ten."

"You look twelve at least," Jared said. "How'd you like to learn a little poker?"

He smoothly shuffled a new deck of red and white cards. Patsy noticed the black specks on his fingers.

Jared explained about pairs, three of a kind, straights, flushes, full houses, and dealt them each a hand. Patsy listened and tried to keep track. Carole and Sharon blew bubbles through their straws.

"Arrange them like this." He spread his cards and showed them what matched, the suits and the colors. "Pairs are the easiest thing to remember," he said, "do you have any pairs?"

"I have two tens," Patsy said.

"Good. What do you want to bet that your cards are better than mine? Got any dimes?"

"I don't have any money," Patsy said. "Neither do Carole or Sharon. We don't get an allowance."

"That's okay; let's play for matches." He tore four each from his matchbook.

They started the game. Sharon and Carole soon lost interest. Only Jared and Patsy played on. Jared picked at the spots on his fingers as he studied his cards.

"What's that black stuff on your hands?" she asked.

"Tar. I'm doing the roof at the Catholic school. Maybe you go there."

"Not me," Patsy said. "I have a friend that does. Sometimes she takes me into the church and we pay a dime to light a candle."

"Is that right?" Jared pulled a black wad from his pocket. "It's fresh tar for chewing. Want to try?"

Patsy slipped a small piece into her mouth. "Not bad," she said, "kind of like gum, only stronger."

They chewed and played cards. Patsy won twice, and she wanted to play more. Each time he dealt new cards, she felt hopeful.

She sneaked looks at Jared. His hair was a faded red, parted on the left side and plastered flat to his skull, and his skin looked like tissue paper. She could see the blue vein in the middle of his forehead and his eyebrows were only as light as a memory.

The rest of the summer was just as hot. The girls would wait a little while in the car, then come in for the nightly card games with Jared.

Patsy and Jared talked about all kinds of things as they studied their cards. He asked about school and if she read Nancy Drew books like his sister. He said he was from North Dakota and had quit school at thirteen to follow the wheat harvest.

"Sometime, I'll take you for an ice cream in my car," he said.

"You're nice." Patsy smiled at him. "You could be our pretend Dad."

"I'm not old," Jared told her. "Not nearly that old."

In August Patsy tasted beer. That great stuff that kept her parents away from home every night.

"Go ahead, have a sip," Audrey said. "You might as well have your first drink here where I can see you."

Patsy took a big swallow. "Yuk. I don't want any more."

Audrey laughed. "I'll get you another Coke."

That night there was a scuffle at the bar. A couple of cowboys left to finish their fight on the sidewalk. Everybody rushed to watch. Patsy seized the chance to use the bathroom that was usually busy. When she came out, Jared stood in the narrow hallway.

"Come on, give us a little kiss," he bent toward her.

She hesitated, but with his eyes closed he looked kind of sweet.

His lips on hers felt soft, like a kitten's nose. The tar smell was strong and she smelled sweat—man sweat. Then he touched her chest.

"Buds." He groaned. "Oh god, you have buds."

Just then Darlene, Audrey's friend, appeared. She yanked Patsy into the bathroom with her. When they returned Darlene whispered something in Audrey's ear.

"Come on, young lady; no more bar for you." Audrey pushed Patsy out the door. "You're going home. And you're staying home."

Chapter Eight

1944

Patsy was fourteen in April of 1944. While everybody talked about the progress of the war, Patsy ducked into the girl's lavatory between classes. She didn't care about the success of American bombing or about school. She'd felt full and about to spill over.

Where was the rose stain of her monthly flow that bloomed on her white cotton panties? Where were the crimson drops in the toilet that swirled to pink—like a paintbrush dipped into water?

She hurried back to class. "Crack and separate the eggs, then let the whites get to room temperature before beating." Miss Snyder, the teacher, waved her eggbeater like she was leading a parade. "This will be your last cake this year, because of sugar rationing."

Patsy was failing Home Ec. Her last angel food cake had looked like it'd been run over by a bicycle and was crunchy with bits of eggshells. It was untouched during the practice tea. Other cakes got sampled while hers sat alone like a dirty-faced orphan.

Why didn't the school have cooking lessons for macaroni and cheese, weenies and beans, tuna casseroles since that's all families ate anyway? What did any of this have to do with her?

There would be no more conversations like this morning.

"Baby, you take such good care of us," Audrey said as she had ambled into the kitchen where Patsy was putting away the Cheerioats, the girls' favorite new cereal.

"Can you fold the laundry after school? I'll be back at seven to make supper." She brought her brush out of her pocket and handed it to Patsy, who gave her mother's dishwater blonde hair practiced strokes and pinned it in a French roll.

"Thanks, baby. Do we have any hamburger?" Audrey asked. "I could make a meatloaf or Sloppy Joes."

Patsy cradled her books and resisted the urge to slam the screen door. That would be the day, she thought. There hadn't been any hamburger in the freezer for months. It held only a few dried packages of ground venison that someone from the bar had brought over at Christmas. Usually she fed the girls canned soup, crackers and Jell-O for supper.

The clock in the classroom seemed stuck. Each minute was like a whole day in Home Ec class. Patsy opened her *Betty Crocker Cookbook* with the wartime cooking supplement, and pretended to scrutinize the recipe for Meatloaf Surprise. The bell finally rang, and she hurried to the bathroom. Nothing. Her next class was her favorite, typing.

With her hands on the keys she felt efficient, in control. Her worry disappeared in the clatter. The class had started typing on covered keys. Looking at the practice book tilted next to their Underwoods, they let their fingers find the letters by memory. Patsy was getting pretty good, except today her hands got started on the wrong keys and she had a sentence of nonsense. *z pir'. Sdjfglak thn benor w;qouen wosskjanb xiotge dj ajsld.*

To calm herself, she settled the pleats on her skirt. For school, she had three pleated skirts and four sweaters she'd bought with her babysitting money. Varying her look with a white lace collar and some fake pearls with matching clip on earrings, she could stretch her outfits. Today, the earrings pinched so she took them off and set them in her lap.

She tried the sentences again looking at her hands, imagining that she was allowed to wear red polish. This time was better. *The quick brown fox jumped over the lazy brown dog,* she typed. *A man must come to the aid of his country.* No errors.

Her shorthand was even better and she imagined herself taking dictation, notebook in her lap, crossed legs in sheer nylons and brown and white spectator pumps on her tiny feet. She might hitch her skirt over one knee if she liked her boss. She couldn't wait to be a secretary. Engrossed, she stayed five minutes after the bell.

"Hi, Patsy." Ronnie Willhagen, her boyfriend, waited on the sidewalk. "What took so long?" He reached for her books. "Can I walk you home?"

Short, stocky, his jeans rolled in thick cuffs, his shirt pressed, his freckles like a sprinkling of sand over his cheeks and ski jump nose—he was a cowlick of a boy. He was so eager and cute; Patsy forgot for a minute what he'd done.

"You can't come in," she told him on the porch. "I have to help Carole with her science project. She's growing beans in a jar."

"Oh, I did that too." He held the door for her. "I started my beans in a wet paper towel. Mine got so tall I named it Ronnie's beanstalk."

Patsy slammed the screen door. She watched him walk away with his head down, scuffing the toes of his shoes. There were no wrinkles in the back of his shirt. She knew, for a fact, that he did his own ironing and was proud of his crisp shirts.

When the girls were in bed, Patsy stood in front of the mirror on her mother's dresser. She stripped to her bra and panties. Her bra was an old one of Audrey's. The tiny blue bow between the cups had faded and the cups had plenty of fabric to expand. Her panties were one size too big; Audrey said she'd grow into them.

Turning sideways, she checked her profile. Her stomach was perfectly flat. She slipped the bra straps off her shoulders and stepped out of her panties. She had narrow hips and her pubic hair was a dark triangle between her legs. With her hands, she tried to circle her waist. They didn't quite meet as usual. Everything looked the same. Except her nipples seemed darker. She leaned into the mirror. Were they bigger? She touched them lightly. They had changed from pale pink to light brown.

Getting chilly, she wrapped in her mother's robe that smelled of burned toast and talcum powder. Lying on the living room sofa, she put her hands on her belly and pressed. Nothing, she felt nothing, although she imagined somewhere deep inside her a beanstalk with one green leaf, reaching, reaching for the light.

⇛⇚

"Ronnie, is that you?" Patsy knew it was. She'd been avoiding him during the two weeks since he'd walked her home from school. He was sitting on the porch swing. Creak, creak, creak, his foot pushed it back and forth.

"Come out," he called.

She slipped out the screen door. They sat in silence at opposite ends of the swing. The breeze rustled the cottonwood and laced the shadows with light. In a week or two the cotton pods would burst and pile up in the gutters like snow.

Ronnie reached for her hand, and she jerked it away. "Are you still mad at me?" he asked.

"I hate you."

"I couldn't help it." His voice got louder. "I just couldn't help it."

"Oh, you could, too. You could have stopped." Patsy glared at him despite his cute freckles and his puppy dog eyes.

The night it happened, Ronnie had come over after supper. It had felt so cozy, like a real family. The girls were in bed. They'd made popcorn and settled on the couch to listen to the radio. They hated *Abbot and Costello,* which was more popular, and listened only to *One Man's Family,* which was ending for the season. Patsy had sent for the book of pictures of the players in their roles and they read it together. Sometimes they pretended they were Henry and Fanny, their favorite characters.

Their making out had been progressing for the last six months. Ronnie had discovered how to unhook her bra with one hand. He was ecstatic with permission to go that far and talked to her breasts like they were goddesses, constantly praising and adoring them.

When his hands strayed lower, she stopped him. "This is the equator," she said and put his hand on the waistband of her skirt. "You don't have a passport for these southern countries."

That night the radio show ended with Henry on one knee proposing to Fanny.

"Happily ever after," the host of the show said, and the opening notes of the wedding march flowed from the radio.

"That's not true," Patsy said. "Are *your* parents happy?"

Ronnie mumbled and kissed her harder, his rough whiskers scratching her cheeks. She pushed him away. Audrey had touched her cheek one morning. "Is that a whisker burn?"

"No, Audrey. Just some pimples."

"Hmm. Looks like one to me," Audrey said.

"I'll just use some Noxzema, and it will be gone by tomorrow."

After that, Ronnie shaved twice a day to please her. However, tonight the beard was back. She'd have to remind him again. He was breathing hard and rocking his hips against her. She slid away from him and her head tilted at a weird angle.

"Oh, sorry." He noticed her discomfort and put one of the couch pillows behind her head. "Is that okay?"

"Better." Now she was flat on her back and he rolled over her. She felt claustrophobic and twisted away. He pinned her. Before she knew it, his hands were under her skirt. He yanked aside her panties and released himself from his jeans. Jamming into her, it was over in a minute or two. Then he left, slamming the screen door behind him. She lay on the couch a long time, watching the sliver of a moon in the living room window.

Ronnie's face had gone pale as skim milk when she announced her pregnancy. His freckles stood out like islands in a white sea. "You are? How do you know?"

"The usual way, Ronnie. I missed my period."

"Jeez, it—it was just that one time. How do you get that way the first time?"

"I throw up every morning, too."

Ronnie worked his finger under his collar. He had on his usual ironed white shirt.

"What are we going to do?"

"I could ask Al. Maybe he knows where you could go."

"Please," Patsy whispered, "don't tell Al. I'm not doing that."

"Maybe you could go away; stay with your Grandma or something. Have it and give it up for adoption."

"Everyone would know. And Audrey—God, Audrey's going to kill me."

"It's her own fault. She should have been home with her kids, instead of leaving you alone every night."

"I knew better." Patsy started to cry. "Now I'm trapped. I don't want to have kids. I want to go to secretarial school."

Ronnie took her hand. "Don't cry—I'll do the right thing by you. We'll get married."

Patsy blew her nose. "Where will we live? Neither of us has any money."

"I'll figure it out. I can get more hours at the cleaners."

"What about school?"

"Hell with it. My uncle wants me to go full time, anyway. You could finish—you only have a few more classes."

"I'm not going to show my face around school." She crossed her arms over her chest. "Jeez, I'd rather die."

"It's not your fault, Patsy." He rubbed his chin. "I should've been more prepared. You know, used a rubber or something."

"It's always the girl's fault, Ronnie, you know that."

The wedding had been at the courthouse. Audrey, Buzzy and Ronnie's mom, Mildred, were the only guests. The parents had to sign so the teens could get the marriage license, and the couple had to get blood tests to prove that they had no venereal diseases. Audrey hadn't been as upset as Patsy expected. Relieved, maybe, one girl married off, two more to go.

Patsy wore a pale blue dotted-Swiss dress. It had a square neckline, lower than she was used to and a yellow sash that tied in the back. Audrey had picked the dress from Vera's, the town's best women's shop, saying, "You should look pretty one last time. And Carole can wear the dress for her graduation."

The newly wed couple moved into Mildred's basement. Not ideal, it was damp and the chenille bedspread smelled like mold. Patsy slept a lot during the day as she often felt nauseous and had nothing else to do. Mildred didn't trust her to do any of the housework.

Ronnie usually worked late at the cleaners and would arrive home just in time for Mildred's suppers. After, the young couple would descend to their corner of the basement. Ronnie always instigated their nightly lovemaking and Patsy would hush him up if he was too loud. Most nights, Patsy would silently cry as Ronnie snored. She missed school, her sisters, and her whole life.

Five months into her marriage, Patsy sat in her own bathtub. She'd gotten in the habit of sneaking home during the day. Buzzy and Audrey were at work, the girls in school. In her own house, she could take her time. At Mildred's they all shared the same bathroom, so she carefully rationed her visits.

She looked at her breasts. What on earth was happening to them? Could they possibly get any bigger? Blue veins crisscrossed each creamy mountain. And her nipples had spread like cookies baking in a hot oven.

She traced another vein that ran down her rounded tummy from her navel to her pubic hair. Her belly button was starting to protrude like a knot in a balloon. She pushed it in. Then she stood in the tub and twisted to examine her rear. Purple stretch marks slashed her buttocks. She'd gained twenty-three pounds already, even though she was only six months. She sank down, her tears dripping into the warm water.

Six weeks later, Patsy had gotten used to the bumping inside her. It became something her very own. When people stared at her in the grocery store, their eyes sliding to her tummy, the movement inside comforted her. Then, something happened.

"I don't feel anything," she told the doctor.

"For how long?" He reached for his stethoscope.

"All weekend. Maybe starting Thursday. What's wrong?" Her voice shook.

He placed the stethoscope on her abdomen. It felt cold. "I don't detect a heartbeat. Hmm, have you had any falls?"

"Not really, I did trip on the basement steps, except I didn't fall hard, or anything."

"Sometimes these things just happen. The cord could have gotten around the neck. Or it wasn't really viable."

"Is there still a baby?" Patsy held her breath.

"This isn't good," he said. "I think it expired." He turned and put his hand on the doorknob. "You'll go into labor in a few days, and it will be over. There'll be other chances for a youngster like you."

She had carried the dead baby for over two weeks. Her stomach shrunk during that time, although people still asked. "When are you due?" Or sometimes they even patted her stomach and smiled at her. Patsy felt numb, and she turned away from Ronnie every night, facing the basement wall. She'd finally delivered after an easy labor, and they let her hold the baby for a moment and then whisked her away.

One day she was surprised to have Meckler at her reading table in the library. He still muttered and more than once called her "little girl, little girl from the car." She wasn't afraid of him anymore. Everything bad seemed to have happened already.

One morning, about a month after delivery, she stood in the basement where their bed and dresser were parked behind an old drape. What should she do now? She walked around the curtain where the shelves of canning jars glowed red and gold in the dim light. She wanted to pull the shelves over, and drench the cold cement floor with mushy fruit and broken glass. Instead, she clutched one jar and ran up the stairs. In the alley behind the house, she slammed it into a neighbor's garbage can.

Later that day, a Help Wanted sign drew her into Ruth's Beauty Shop. Buzzy had said they didn't need anyone at the café. Just as well, Patsy thought, she didn't feel like being around her parents. She was tired of answering questions. She didn't want to see Carole and Sharon. They were so innocent, lively and young. With them, she felt old and hollow.

"Can you start tomorrow?" Ruth asked. She had iron-gray hair, a slim body and a brusque contralto voice. "It will only be until the other operator comes back. Have you had any experience?"

"Not yet. I can type sixty words a minute and take shorthand."

"The job will be cleaning up and washing hair."

"I'm good at that." Patsy remembered how many times she'd scrubbed her sisters' hair with the three of them standing in the tin shower. And how Audrey would lean back in the kitchen chair with her head in the sink for Patsy to shampoo.

"Your application looks okay. I'll see you in the morning."

Years later, standing at her own shop door, Patsy remembered that she'd stayed home in charge of her sisters after the incident in the bar, although it hadn't kept her out of trouble as a teen. In fact, it was at home where her biggest problem had begun. Would it help Bobbi to talk with her? She turned the key in the trailer door. At the moment, she had no answers.

Chapter Nine

1958

"Bobbi, phone for you."

It was Rita. Only part of her sentence served, and Bobbi felt desperate for company. Rita said her Grandma was there, which was their code for having your period. So, Rita couldn't come over. And Donna, Rita added, was working on her history paper.

Unlike Bobbi, both girls lucked out with no punishment from the car trip with the teacher. Rita's mother was late that night too, as she had been cleaning the church. And Donna by some miracle convinced her parents she was actually working on a school project.

It was Friday night, and she was alone. She felt doomed. Did Donna and Rita even care? Maybe they were dropping her. She thought about everything she hated about them—like when Rita peed in their sleeping bag on an overnight, and the smell lasted forever. And at a slumber party she'd spied Donna slipping her thumb into her mouth. And how Donna forgot to bring her toothbrush to camp, and after three days Bobbi caught Donna sneaking hers. Truly icky girls.

They'd all gone on the drive to Fort Peck together, so what had changed? Was it about the bitchin' teacher's car they were desperate to drive? Or just to be with the new teacher. They were jealous of each other now!

She used to play with Rita and Donna every day. Donna lived just three houses down. Rita became her friend in first grade; she'd called the teacher when Bobbi fell off the monkey bars.

Summer mornings they'd come to her door when the grass was still wet. The three of them would run down her hill, neighing like horses. Back then, they never quarreled or said mean things about each other like they'd had lately.

Donna's hair was so blonde, it looked white, and Rita had a jumble of dark curls, and Bobbi was a brunette, so they thought they looked perfect together.

Their moms would hand them sack lunches, and they'd play all day—weaving their bikes through hedges, sidewalks and alleys. Every afternoon they'd ask for nickels to buy Popsicles at Green Front Grocery. Choosing the flavor—grape or lime took long minutes. They'd sit on the curb sucking the frozen treats, and licking long drips from their dusty arms.

Long summer days would end with sleeping outdoors, and dashing through yards with flashlights blinking like lightening bugs. They'd steal carrots from backyard gardens, licking the dirt and chewing loud like horses. One night while clad in their pj's, they walked the warm sidewalks to the outskirts of town, where they perched on the edge of a freshly dug hole that waited for a cement foundation. Their feet dangled in air as the night sky wheeled overhead, and the Northern Lights waved curtains of green. Bobbi remembered feeling very small, yet unafraid.

Out of her fog of memory, Bobbi stared at the kitchen clock. It was only eight. What was she going to do all night? She felt abandoned, and her stomach hurt. Was she going to start her period?

In her closet she climbed atop her dresser and pushed open the trapdoor to the attic. Feeling around in the insulation, she pulled down the dusty book. On her last visit to the library, she'd slipped it into her book bag from the Adult's Only bookshelf. By flashlight she'd been reading it under her covers at night. The author was Frank Yerby, who wrote steamy romances.

A Woman Called Fancy. She read the blurb on the back of the book.

"Men offered everything they possessed to possess her—but there was only one man she wanted. From him she asked only love."

Bobbi wrapped her arms around her chest in a tight hug. Yes, she only wanted love from Pretty Weasel, even if he had showered her with gifts. Just love, even if he had nothing! What would love like that feel like?

She didn't really feel like reading and hid the book under her mattress. Then she wandered around the house, looking out the windows, hoping there was something going on. Wishing she could talk to Donna and Rita about the dirty parts of the book—and about love.

When they were young, Donna, Rita and Bobbi discussed everything. They were never bored and played with all the kids— boys, too—with none of the self-consciousness Bobbi felt now. Another favorite pastime, she recalled, was hiking to the cemetery. They'd touch the stone lambs on the baby's headstone and sob, pretending they were the sisters of the dead.

Those summers with her friends were a fond memory, but she'd also had more punishments in the summer. When her dad traveled for work, her mom was touchy. She spanked the girls with the hairbrush, bristle side to their little girl legs.

When dad arrived home with his tired brown eyes and tan muscled arms, Bobbi followed him around like a puppy. She loved him so much, though he hardly ever had time for her, or Marlene, or even her mom. When he had headaches, terrible migraines, they tiptoed around the house with the shades pulled.

Her best memory was the summer she was nine. "Look," Bobbi had said, "Dad made me stilts!"

She clumped around the driveway.

"Can I try?" Donna put her feet on the pegs and fell when her legs got too far apart.

"Here." Bobbi showed her how to start by leaning against the garage door. "That's so much better."

"Me?" Rita said and took a turn.

They played on the stilts all day, stumping around yards, and up and down the outside stairs. After the girls left that day, Bobbi sat on the steps. The DDT truck rumbled through the alley and sprayed the pungent mist into the dark air. She loved summer—it went on and on like a journey across a lake without seeing the distant shore. And she loved her friends.

Chapter Ten

Where were her friends now? Bobbi was sick and tired of being grounded. *Jesus God*, she hated missing the action on a Friday night. She checked the homework handout from Miss Bauer that included her phone number. "Call me sometime, Bobbi," she'd said.

"Number, please," the operator asked.

Bobbi tried to disguise her voice, as the operators knew about everything going on in town. She didn't want her calls to the teacher getting back to her dad. She gripped the phone in one sweaty hand and then the other. It rang ten times with no answer. *Double damn!* Although, what would she say, anyway?

Green stamps! She'd forgotten about the collection of stamps they got when they shopped for groceries and gas. She raced to the kitchen. From a drawer, she pulled out loose stamps and books. It wasn't clear that the books belonged to Bobbi. But, why not? She was the injured party.

She riffled the catalog. A pale blue train case with a mirror on the inside lid snagged her attention. She'd sell her soul for it, but it was twenty-seven books. Her stash was nineteen.

A variety of kitchen gadgets were displayed in the well-worn pages. A set of mixing bowls in red, yellow and turquoise; matching BBQ aprons for her mom and dad; a white breadbox with colorful pictures of peanut butter and pimento loaf sandwiches. No, no, and no. Finally, a cherry red Ice-O-Mat Ice Crusher, hand cranked with fine and extra fine settings caught her eye. That she could use! Imagine pouring grape Kool-Aid over a tall glass of crushed ice and offering it to her friends. Monday, she'd mail them in.

Now what? Everyone else in the world had something to do on Friday night at eight, even the parents. She could picture them drinking their favorite scotch and bragging about their new Pontiacs as they slobbered over steaks.

Mom and Dad hadn't seemed to care that she'd be alone or that she could sneak out if she felt like it. So when Marlene left, she followed her to Bev's house. It made her jealous that they'd giggle, read movie magazines and try on each other's bras. Once she sneaked Marlene's bra, the one with the lace trim. Of course, it was way too big.

She watched Bev's house for a while. Then she killed more time by playing hopscotch on the sidewalk. All at once she heard screeching and saw the convertible careen around the corner. The driver looked frightened by the squeal of the tires. It was Rita. *Dammit to hell and back!* She couldn't believe it. Rita had never driven before. Donna was in the back, and Miss Bauer was riding shotgun, a glowing cig in her hand.

With her heart pounding, she ducked into the thimbleberry bushes, and crouched in the dirt. Had they seen her? *Shit, purple shit.* So that's why they couldn't come over. Not only were they with Jean, they got to drive!

She tasted sick and thrust her hand over her mouth to keep from barfing. *Those dirty double-crossers!* Was this how Jesus felt? She was the one with the license—she should have been the first driver! Instead, she was betrayed, first by one Judas, then another.

The rest of the weekend felt as long as a summer when she was nine, only not in a good way. Neither Rita nor Donna rang her, and she would rather sew up her mouth with Grandma's darning needle than call them. Twice she phoned Miss Bauer and hung up when she answered.

Saturday morning, while her mom was out, she decided to learn to smoke. That would show them! She sat in the living room determined to inhale or die, and lit a Pall Mall. *Disgusting.* She coughed and coughed while spitting bits of tobacco, then raced to the kitchen for water. She smoked five more, gently tapping the ashes into her mom's crystal ashtray, until she got dizzy and her breakfast orange juice burned in her throat. Finally, lying on the couch, she put one foot on the floor to steady the room.

On Monday she wore her new Pendleton skirt to school that she'd been saving for the first sock hop. It had taken her a summer of babysitting to pay for it. And she sneaked Marlene's lace collar.

"Cute skirt," Donna said.

"Thanks." Bobbi dug a bent cig from her purse.

"You're smoking? In school?" Rita shrilled.

"Oh, sure." Bobbi expertly blew smoke through her nostrils. "Love one before class."

"Want to come over after school?" Donna asked. "We could make Rice Krispies Treats."

"No." Bobbi took the gum wrappers from her purse and dropped them one by one in the garbage can. "I have to finish my history paper."

Donna and Rita exchanged looks in the mirror.

"It's not due until Thursday, and you know how I like to get things done ahead of time." Bobbi turned toward the door. "Just like you, Donna, when you stayed home last Friday night to do your history paper."

Rita dropped her lipstick in the sink. It made a scarlet trail.

Bobbi retrieved it. "Your point is ruined."

"Oh, fudge!" Rita capped the flattened lipstick. She and Donna again locked eyes. "How'd you know we were with Miss Bauer?"

"I saw you driving her car!"

"Thought you were grounded. Anyway, we wanted to ask you, except you had to stay home. And Miss Bauer said *we* could drive."

"Sure." Bobbi said, "No problem. I don't know when I can see you guys—I'm starting to work at the beauty shop, and I'll probably get a new hairdo. Plus, I've been on the phone all weekend," she cracked her gum, "with a cute guy."

After English class Bobbi stood by her desk. "Miss Bauer," she asked, "can you recommend any other books by Salinger? I loved *Catcher,* although Rita and Donna hated it."

Miss Bauer grinned. Her hair looked cleaner today. "You read fast."

"I do?" She shifted her books to the other arm. "I'll read whatever you suggest."

"I'll work up a book list for you. Extra credit, of course."

"I'm on my way to the library right now. Reading's my favorite thing, next to driving, of course. I have a learner's permit."

"You like to drive? I have a teacher's meeting now. Can we meet at five? Come by my apartment, number three, the building behind the Dairy Queen."

"Uh . . ." Bobbi was supposed to be home at five to set the table and make the cream cheese and pineapple salad. "Sure, no problem."

Rita and Donna stood near her locker. "Bobbi, what's going on?"

"Nothing." She spun her padlock.

"Who's calling you? The mysterious boy?" Donna asked. "Are you making it up?"

"And what were you discussing with Miss Bauer?" Rita pushed next to Bobbi.

"Oh, he's real all right! We might have a date for the weekend." She fluffed her hair. "Miss Bauer, Jean, offered me extra credit. We are meeting later." Bobbi spoke over her shoulder. "At her place."

Rita stepped forward. "Can we go?"

"She only invited me. *Sorry.*"

Bobbi had never been in an apartment. All her friends lived in houses. In the front room sat a brown tweed sofa, and a bookshelf with a radio. A small chrome dinette crouched under the window by the tiny kitchen. Behind a half-closed door she glimpsed an unmade bed. She imagined it looked like a motel room. No pictures, no plants, no doilies.

Miss Bauer wore blue jeans, a man's white shirt and penny loafers with no socks. A kinda cool outfit, Bobbi thought as she perched on the sofa. She tried not to look at the car keys and the cookies on the table. Her stomach rumbled. It had been a long time since her lunch.

"So, you always have your nose in a book?" Jean asked.

"Yes. I sneak library books from the Adult Only section. Last week I read *Native Son,* the week, before *Lolita.* "

"When I was your age, I devoured everything in the library, even the baseball stories. Did you ever read, *The Boy Who Batted 1000?*"

"No."

"Oreos?" Jean slit open the new pack.

"Well—maybe one, then I better get home. What time is it?"

Jean turned her wrist to check. She wore the watch face on the inside of her wrist.

"Wait, before you go. I'll give you another lesson." She rolled back her shirtsleeves. Bobbi had never seen such sinewy arms on a woman. Why did they have to do the tickle thing again? This wasn't fun like they'd had at the lake. She wished her friends were here.

"Now lean back on the couch. When I start, look at the doorknob."

"The *doorknob*?"

"It's called dissociating—removing yourself from the situation. Look at anything you want, except at me."

The sofa felt as hard as the bleachers. Scratchy, too. Bobbi gazed at a scuff mark on the bedroom door. She started a story in her mind about how a murderer tried to break the door down.

The fingers worked on her ribs, while she stayed on her story. Quickly, it was too much—she felt smothered by the arms and probing hands, and she squirmed away.

"You did really well." Jean said. "We can practice again."

Bobbi jumped up. "I *have to* go."

"So soon?"

"I'm on KP tonight."

"Too bad." Jean moved closer. "Friday I'm going to Williston for a basketball game. I'd love some company if it's okay with your parents."

"Overnight?" Bobbi's mind jumped to the possibility of telling Donna and Rita that she had a date on Friday night. Especially, as there was no boy who'd been calling. "I want to. But . . ."

"You could drive. With the top down."

Bobbi pictured herself in the car. Driving by Williston High School on the smooth red leather seats, the envy of all the kids flowing over her like chocolate syrup. It made her mouth water.

Jean slipped a Pall Mall into the corner of her mouth, "Let me know. Otherwise, I'll ask Donna or Rita. They're getting to be such good drivers."

"I have my learner's permit, and they don't." Bobbi closed the apartment door behind her.

Bobbi slipped in the kitchen door after six, expecting to catch holy hell for being late. Instead, she heard the girls in Marlene's bedroom whispering and they stopped when she barged in.

"What's going on? Where are the lovely parents?"

Marlene said, "That's for us to know and you to find out." She had a plate of saltine crackers and an open bag of chocolate chips on the bed.

Bobbi reached for the chocolate. "I'm starved. Aren't we having dinner?"

"Just make one of your icky sandwiches." Marlene pushed her to the door. "Don't use all the marshmallows!"

Bobbi carried her peanut butter and marshmallow sandwich to her room. The house felt strangely empty. Where was her mom? She played a few records, put on gobs of blue eye shadow and rubbed it off, and then sat in the kitchen waiting.

What in *holy hell* was going on? No supper, no Dad.

About eight-thirty, her mom came home and said Bobbi could have a bowl of Grape-Nuts for dinner. She added, "I'm going out with Mag. I shouldn't be home too late."

"It's already nine. Where's Dad?"

"Reffing somewhere. And it's your bedtime, young lady."

Dying with curiosity, Bobbi waited until Mag picked up her mom, then hopped in the station wagon and followed them. Mag dropped her mom behind the Montana where she slipped into the front seat of a blue Buick. She couldn't see the driver—although, she couldn't miss the way her mom slid next to him. *Christ on a cracker*, were they making out?

Afraid to see any more, she sped home. She put on her pj's, brushed her teeth, and got in bed without her flashlight and library book. Someone needed to follow the rules.

About ten she was still awake and sweaty under the heavy quilt. When she heard a noise, she eased out of bed and crept to the kitchen. There were no vampires, as she had imagined, only Gwen, their tabby cat, on the kitchen counter licking the butter dish.

"Get down, you bad cat!"

Hearing gravel crunch, she peeked out the back window. The car crouched like a sleeping buffalo in the alley. Was that Duffy's car? One shape loomed in the front seat for a long time, and then a car door quietly closed. Her mom dashed into the kitchen.

With lipstick gone, wrinkled capris, blouse loose, cheeks flushed like the Thanksgiving she'd drunk too much Mogen David wine, she'd never seen her mom look so sparkly and young.

"Bobbi, for God's sake! You scared me. Why aren't you in bed?" She thrust her hands into the sink and splashed her face with cold water.

Chapter Eleven

"Hi, Bobbi, I'm Patsy Olson." She offered her hand. "Your dad said you're a good worker."

"Really?" Bobbi doubted that. He probably said she was good slave labor. She gave Patsy a limp handshake. *Why did she have to work for this floozy?*

"Your job will be to shampoo the ladies." She lowered her voice. "I call them heads. And to sweep up the hair, keep the sink and toilet clean. A buck an hour."

"Toilet?" Bobbi gave her a stare. Patsy's blonde hair was teased into a bubble shape with small pink bows clipped to each side. She was short, her tight curves like a racetrack. Her wide blue eyes seemed to expand when they looked at you. Her pink smock matched her smooth pink lips and glossy fingernails. Her feet were squeezed into pink kitten heels. Bobbi didn't have to guess the color of her panties.

"Here's the broom. Sweep up the hair."

"Okay." *Cripes*, she thought, *this wasn't going to be fun.*

She watched Patsy's hands move like lightning. Comb, roll in the curler and fasten with a pick. The curlers were pink, of course. She sat Mildred in the dryer chair and pulled down the hood.

"I did eight heads today," she told Bobbi. "I can do five more with your help."

Patsy patted her own hair like it was something precious and rare. Bobbi thought it looked like a swimming cap.

Patsy lit a cig and blew the smoke out her nostrils like Betty Davis.

"Do you smoke?" she asked.

"No."

"Oh, come on, all teenagers smoke. It's okay—I won't tell your dad."

Right, she's just leading me on, Bobbi thought. "I'll get started on the cleaning. At five I have to meet my science teacher."

Patsy leaned into the mirror to put on more eyeliner and lipstick. *As if she needed more makeup,* Bobbi thought.

"You're fourteen, right?"

"Yup, a lowly freshman."

"The teens—that was a bad time for me."

"Why?" It seemed impossible to Bobbi that anyone on the grown-up planet had been a teen.

"Forget about it. Unless you want to hear about a kid that didn't make it." She was dead—a baby girl, Patsy said to herself. She reached for the combs. "Want me to do something with your hair?"

"Like what?" Bobbi asked.

"Trim your bangs. Did you cut them with pinking shears?"

"No."

Bobbi dumped the cleanser in the sink and toilet. While waiting for it to work, she checked her profile and the back of her head in the hand mirror. After all, this was the view most people had of her. Ugh. Her nose jutted like Mt. Rushmore. Why couldn't she have a perky little nose like Sandra Dee? Her bangs were crooked. Maybe they did need a touch-up.

She checked the medicine cabinet. Tampax. Stored in a plastic box, pink, of course. Regular size. She and Donna laughed about who would use the super. Anyway, she couldn't use Tampax yet—she hadn't started her period and she was still a virgin.

Her stupid sister, Marlene, and her friend Sheila had a pool with their friends. Each had a quarter on the day they thought Bobbi would start her period. The supplies waited in her bottom drawer under her pj's. She'd practiced hooking the giant Kotex pads to the elastic belt. She wasn't looking forward to the waddly thing between her legs every month for the rest of her life, and worse, she didn't want to leave toilet paper bundles in the wastebasket.

Their Physical Ed teacher had explained about menstruation and all that stuff. On the blackboard she drew a uterus and ovaries. Then she drew the man's thing. Bobbi swore it looked just like a plump hot dog. No one in the class moved as the teacher started to explain the good part—how the hot dog got in. Just then the hall monitor, a boy, had entered with the attendance slip. Miss Peabody dropped her chalk. The girls held their breath as he'd glanced at the blackboard, then rushed out with a red face.

One morning Bobbi had seen the worst of it. As she was brushing her teeth, Marlene came into the bathroom. The front of her nightie was soaked—crimson color staining the flannel. Bobbi had never seen anything like it. Was her sister dying? "It's only the curse," Marlene said. "You'll get it, too.

Bobbi left the trailer bathroom to sweep up gobs more hair. Funny, the ladies were discussing what she'd been thinking about.

"I've been flooding for a week. About ten pads a day," one said.

"Better than being late," the other customer chuckled. "Did you ever think you'd look forward to cramps?"

"Did you ever think you'd have the Pope in your bedroom?"

They looked at Bobbi. Sweep, sweep, she kept her head down.

"The rhythm method," the lady said. "What a joke. I'd have eight kids if Tommy ran out of rubbers."

Bobbi didn't know about the rhythm method, however, she knew about rubbers. During a football game, she was under the bleachers picking up empty pop bottles, because Green Front Grocery paid a nickel each. She discovered a wallet with a Trojan in it. She slipped it in her pocket before she turned the wallet in. Later, in Donna's bedroom, they opened the foil package and examined their prize. It looked like a skinny balloon. They dared each other to blow it up.

In a break, Patsy said. "It's a big job running this place. I'm glad to have the help." She unwrapped a piece of gum. "Want one?"

Bobbi took a stick. "I guess you can do my bangs." She plopped in the styling chair.

"I have time before the comb outs." Patsy worked carefully with her scissors, although her mind was on a visitor she'd had earlier. Mag had stopped by and asked Patsy for a favor, but it'd felt more like a demand.

"I've put together bingo prizes for the Indians," Mag had announced. "We hope to keep them off the highways at night by organizing bingo games with good prizes. Would you contribute?"

"Of course, happy to help," Patsy had lied. She couldn't afford a cash donation. "What can I do?"

"A free haircut every week."

Patsy tightened the cap on a bottle of bleach. "I've never done Indian hair."

"I've seen your work, you'll have no problem. I thought you'd agree, so I put you down for this week. My cleaning lady, Mary Agnes Lone Hill, won. She'll drop by."

Mag gave a little wave. "Gotta go, thanks!"

"*Voilà!*" Patsy twirled the styling chair so Bobbi could look in the mirror.

Bobbi touched her bangs. "They look better, thanks." Patsy might look cheap, Bobbi thought, except she seemed nice, and she did do a super job on her hair. She couldn't wait to show Donna and Rita. Maybe there was hope for her looks after all.

There was a quiet knock on the door.

"It's open," Patsy called.

Mary Agnes stepped in. She wore her usual outfit—a baggy white shirt, rumpled jeans, and rundown shoes. Her black hair was in a messy braid.

"Mrs. Henderson said I should come here for a haircut."

Edna, from under her hooded hair dryer, poked Mildred.

"My stars," Mildred said.

Patsy bustled over. "You must be Mary Agnes Lone Hill. Sit here." She gestured to an empty chair "I'll get to you in a minute."

Today? *Jesus H. Christ,* couldn't Mrs. Henderson have given her a little time to prepare? She didn't need another problem. But, from the looks on Edna's and Mildred's faces, she needed to get them out quickly. She pulled Edna from under the dryer and started her comb out.

"Bobbi," she said, "can you take the curlers out of Mildred's hair?"

"Okay," Bobbi answered.

Instead of the usual chatter, the place was quiet. It felt stifling, like there wasn't enough air for everyone. No one was making eye contact. The ladies studied their magazines, and Mary Agnes stared at her feet.

Patsy's mind raced with each stroke of the brush. How would this bingo prize work? A free Indian hair cut each week while keeping her regular customers happy would be a high-wire balancing act.

Mrs. Henderson and her friends had husbands to support them while they played bridge and got their hair done. They didn't have a clue about the hours every day she spent on her feet, the bulging blue veins hidden under her nylons, the nights she'd pored over the books, how little money she actually made, and how one whiff of gossip could shut her down.

She felt sorry for Mary Agnes. It took courage to come here, and she really needed a haircut. The poor woman had to clean for a living, and she could bet that Mrs. Henderson didn't pay much.

How to handle the Indian clients was something she needed to think about. The word "Indian" was hardly ever used without the preface "dirty," and she didn't want *that* connected to her place.

She finished both comb-outs and grabbed the appointment book.

"Same time next week?"

"I'll call," Mildred said as she and Edna hurried out.

"Be right back." Patsy ran after them.

"Hold on," she said. "What's the problem?"

"Heavens to Betsy! Don't they have their own place?" Edna whispered.

"You don't have to whisper." Patsy frowned. "She can't hear you. Come back next week for your regular appointment. I'll make sure there are no Indians in the shop."

"I've never heard of such a thing," Edna said.

"It won't happen again."

Bobbi and Mary Agnes were chatting when Patsy came back.

"Guess what?" Bobbi looked excited.

"What now?" Patsy asked. She didn't need any more surprises today.

"Pretty Weasel, one of our really good ball players, she's his mom."

"Great. *Just great.*" Patsy motioned for Mary Agnes to sit in the styling chair.

"What do you have in mind? A new style?"

"I don't know," Mary Agnes mumbled. "I've never had a real haircut."

"Tell you what. Why don't I give it a good wash and shape it up. Get rid of those split ends."

"Okay." Mary Agnes kept her head down.

Patsy unbraided her hair.

Bobbi sat in the styling chair and watched. This was Pretty Weasel's mom? They couldn't be more different. Pretty Weasel was tall, handsome, and sure of himself, Mary Agnes was short, pudgy and shy.

"My gosh, your hair's so long. Have you been growing it forever? How about doing a French braid?" Bobbi fired questions at her. Then she pretended she was dribbling a basketball.

"Where did Pretty Weasel learn to play? My dad's his coach, you know."

"He's a good boy, don't you think?" Mary Agnes asked.

The talk swirled around Patsy while she skillfully cut Mary Agnes's straight black hair. It was all about basketball. Bobbi and Mary Agnes seemed to hit it off. Bobbi was so animated, and Mary Agnes no longer seemed like the timid woman who'd come into the shop. She told Bobbi that she'd played basketball, too.

"He's good, and he got that from me," Mary Agnes said.

"Wow, where did you play?" Bobbi asked.

"Bowman Junior High. We were champs." Mary Agnes smiled at herself in the mirror.

"Really? Tell me about it. And I want to know everything about him. Where was he born? How did he get his name?"

"He was born here. Now he lives in Killdeer with his 'other mother'."

"He taught me to shoot free throws and called me, 'Chokecherry Girl.'"

"Maybe he'll pick you for a girlfriend."

"Has he mentioned me?" Bobbi stood taller. "Does he have a steady?"

Mary Agnes scratched a rough spot on her arm. "Don't know."

"You know what?" Bobbi put her hand over her mouth and whispered, "I'm going to drive a convertible. It'd be neat if I could give Pretty Weasel a ride someday after practice."

Patsy capped a bottle of Wave Set. "Tell you what, Bobbi. Why don't you and Mary Agnes continue your conversation outside? I have some calls to make."

Patsy wanted to be by herself. She needed to think about how she would make sure that the bingo prize foisted off on her wouldn't ruin her business.

A scandal could screw up her reputation. In fact, that's how she'd lost her job a year ago in Malta. The threat remained real—Axel had hurt her before and it could happen again.

Tossing her brushes into the sink, she sank into a chair, put her aching feet up and lit a cigarette.

Chapter Twelve

Mary Agnes and Bobbi sat on the trailer steps. Although it was chilly at four-thirty, the spring sun warmed their faces. Bobbi had already asked her a lot of questions. Mary Agnes didn't want to tell Bobbi that she gave up Pretty Weasel or be reminded of the fact.

"I'll tell you about my Grandma Lillian Turns Plenty, and when I lived with her," Mary Agnes said.

Bobbi laughed. "That's a weird name."

"Not for an Indian. She liked to drive the wagon in circles. She had gray braids and smoked a pipe. Her shack was on the Milk River in the center of the Crow reservation. It was just one room that smelled like wood smoke and sage. "

"Why'd you live with your Grandma?"

Mary Agnes shook her head. "I had questions, too. About my name, and how I got there. Grandma didn't talk much about the past. She said my clan uncle picked Lone Hill, and my mother added Mary Agnes."

"Where *was* your mom?"

"I asked Grandma that all the time. According to her, my mom was one bad Indian."

"My mom's pretty bad, too," Bobbi said.

"Really? I thought white families were so perfect. Does your mom drink?"

Bobbi lowered her voice. "I saw her go into the Montana Bar the other night."

"Are you *sure*? I've never seen a white woman there."

"I was spying on her. Maybe I'm wrong; I don't want to think about her. What did your Grandma say about your mom?"

Mary Agnes paused. "She left with a guy for a Sun Dance in St. Ignatius and never came back."

"Do you remember her?"

"I was real little. It's like looking at a black and white photo. I see a young woman wearing a cowboy hat and a cocky smile."

"Do you miss her? I'd be perfectly fine without my mother." Bobbi gave her leg a slap. "Better off!"

"Grandma taught me how to make chokecherry jelly, how to pickle fruits, and about Old Coyote. Our ancestors used chokecherries in their pemmican and for sickness."

"My grandma makes chokecherry jelly, too. Honestly, she'd pickle anything that grew—watermelon, crab apples, cucumbers."

"The jelly was good on our corn cakes," Mary Agnes said. "I learned Crow Legends from her and how Old Coyote could help us or trick us. Crows believe he made the world."

"I wish my mom would teach me something useful, besides how to iron. I started on the hankies and pillowcases. I've graduated to shirts. Whoopie."

"What's your dad like?" Mary Agnes asked.

"Oh, he's pretty busy. He watches out for me when he can. In fact, he got me this job."

"My dad died in a car crash before I was born." Mary Agnes wiped her nose with her sleeve. "I miss Grandma a lot. Even though she called me a bad Indian sometimes, I know she loved me."

"Is she still alive?"

Mary Agnes pulled her fingers through her shiny clean hair. "She's gone to the 'land of the other-side people.'"

"That's sad."

"I remember a day we spent together. We put up our teepee like Old Coyote taught her. She anchored the poles and pulled out the sides and had me pound the stakes. The pounding felt good, and it sounded like singing. Finally, we finished and crawled inside. It was dark and cool. Grandma groaned when she fell asleep. I didn't know she was sick."

"That's so cool! I love to make tents and sleep outside!"

"I stayed with Grandma all day in the tent. It was like a yellow dream world. I studied the painted sun, the elk with the big antlers, and the hunter with bow and arrow. I turned slowly in a circle." Mary Agnes hopped off the step with her arms out.

"Like this?" Bobbi grabbed Mary Agnes's shoulders and spun her faster and faster.

"Yes," Mary Agnes gasped.

Bobbi turned also. With their arms out like helicopter blades, they whirled, bumping shoulders and laughing until they collapsed.

Mary Agnes caught her breath. "That's exactly how it happened in the tent. As I twirled the elk seemed to be moving, running away from the hunter. The sun moved away from the elk until the elk and the hunter seemed to race the sun. I got so dizzy, I finally fell down and slept. That was my last day with Grandma."

The sun was already down and the streetlights clicked on when Mary Agnes finished. Both were quiet. Bobbi realized she didn't know anything about the Indians, although she'd been around them all her life. Nobody talked about the Crows, except to condemn their drinking and be saddened by their highway dead, who were memorialized by white crosses on the side of the highway.

Bobbi looked at the Indian woman with new eyes. At first she'd felt impatient because she wanted to hear about Pretty Weasel. As Mary Agnes talked more, she got interested in the story of the little girl and her grandma with the odd name. Mary Agnes was a person, too. Not just Pretty Weasel's mom.

"Aren't you dying to know about your mom?" Bobbi asked.

"Not anymore. I feel like she's gone to the 'other side people,' too.'" Mary Agnes brushed the tendrils from her sweaty face. "Sorry, I didn't talk about Pretty Weasel."

"It's okay. I liked hearing about your Grandma. You can tell me about him another time."

After Bobbi left, Mary Agnes hitched a ride back to her place, Grandma's shack. For the first time, she realized how junky it looked with car parts, oil cans, and old bed springs tossed out back. When did this happen? What if Pretty Weasel or Bobbi came by for a visit? She frantically tossed the smaller stuff into the river and piled up the larger items for Ben to haul away.

Chapter Thirteen

1940

After Grandma went to the "land of the other-side people," she'd lived with her Aunt Judy Feather-maker in town. She'd liked school and loved being on the basketball team with her friends, Wanda, Gail and Dede. Then, she'd abruptly been sent away.

She remembered leaving Bowman on the train, and how'd she kicked the seat in front of her where a uniformed soldier sat. Why should she care about scuffed black oxfords or if she offended a guy who'd joined up to fight for his country? After all, she was being sent to an Indian School.

Why did the BIA pick on her? She'd had good grades. It must have been when she got involved with Gail Fast Horse. Gail knew all the kids from the rez. Sometimes they stayed in the park late at night, sitting in the grass playing mumblety-peg. Mary Agnes could beat the boys even in the half-light.

One night, Frank's older brother brought beer. He'd said he was joining up if Roosevelt got them in the war, so they better drink up now. They'd sipped the frothy liquid and taken turns burping. When Mary Agnes held the can it was cold, her lips felt the cold and she pushed it closer to her lips and the frothy liquid spread in her mouth and some wet got in her nose and it stung. Then Frank took away the can, and suddenly, she wanted more, and she licked the small amount of foam in the corner of her mouth and waited.

The can circled and it was shiny and silver dark, and hands clutched it and held it and she watched, as it got nearer. It tasted bad, but good and she wanted more and felt sad when Frank took it out of her hand. She kept waiting and drinking until her tongue poked into the can and it hurt and someone said "look at her" and laughed, and they all laughed and her hand was in Frank's hand and they fell back on the ground. Their hands pumped the air and it had felt like music and their arms and feet moved to the song, the song everywhere, in their legs too, and they were dancing. "Grass dancing," Mary Agnes said, "we're grass dancing."

A week later the BIA agent sat in Aunt Judy's kitchen.

"We've made arrangements for Mary Agnes to attend eighth grade at an Indian School. It starts in August. She'll do better there."

"I don't want her to go."

"Now, Judy, we at the BIA know what's best. You can't keep her here."

Aunt Judy shrugged. She knew that the BIA had complete jurisdiction over any Indian child. "I done the best I could with her, only she's one of those night kids. They drink beer and don't come home."

She picked up an empty pack of cigarettes. "Got a smoke?" When the agent shook his head, she went on. "If I got paid all my lease money, I could've sent her to summer camp. Maybe you want to help an old Indian out."

"Always looking for a hand-out. You people. If you have questions about the lease money, come to the agency. Mary Agnes will be home in a couple of years." The agent pushed the form across the table for her to sign.

It was late afternoon before Mary Agnes ventured to the train bathroom, two cars away. For hours she stayed in her seat, trying not to be noticed. Finally, she whispered to the conductor. "Where's the girls' lavatory?"

On the way to the toilet, she spotted three Indian kids. She wondered if they were being sent away, too. However, she couldn't bring herself to talk to them.

She leaned her head against the window. The cool glass quieted her swirling thoughts. The telephone poles flashed by, faster and faster, the thin wire stretching her farther and farther from home. She imagined leaving a word, one on each pole. The words would be like crumbs left in the forest by Hansel and Gretel. She could follow them back home. She left basketball, Auntie, Wanda, Star Boy, Grandma, knife, chokecherry, feather, beer, and grass dancing.

She recognized the Fords, Buicks and Chevys on the adjacent highway. It reminded her of Auntie's old Hudson and the day when she, Wanda, Gail and Dede had crammed in the big-as-a-cave backseat after a basketball game. They'd giggled and wrote their boyfriends' initials on the steamy windows. When Auntie had spun donuts in the snow, they'd screamed their delight.

The strangest sight from the train was a man on a single wheel bike. He waited at the railroad crossing, wheeling back and forth for balance. Just as the train swept by, he crashed into the gravel.

At sunset, she opened the second paper sack labeled *supper*. The lights went off at nine, and the passengers settled themselves with blankets and pillows. The lone soldier staggered down the aisle, and whispered something rude as he passed. She tried to stay awake in case the soldier came back, although she was dozing when the conductor shook her shoulder.

"You change here."

The train chugged away, leaving the Indian children on the platform. Mary Agnes stood next to her cardboard box and shivered. Her breath puffed small clouds into the frosty air. A single bulb dangled from the station roof, making a small pool of yellow on the platform. Bats swooped in and out of the light. The station was locked for the night, and the children stood there numb with cold.

The boy pulled two girls to the bench. "Sit here, and keep warm. You, too." He gestured to Mary Agnes. "I'm Leo and these are my sisters, Karen and Margaret. We're Blackfeet from the Rocky Boy's Indian Reservation."

Mary Agnes moved to the bench. "I'm Mary Agnes Lone Hill, a Crow from Bowman, Montana. Do you know where we're headed?"

"Nebraska," Leo said. "I saw our tickets. We're going to an Indian boarding school."

"Why are you guys going? Did you get in trouble?"

Leo laughed. "Our dad screwed up. He's in jail. He has to enlist when he gets out, so we have no one to live with. I bet we could have done okay on our own like the boxcar kids."

"*The Boxcar Children,*" Mary Agnes said. "It's only a book. The BIA would hunt us down like wolves. They round us up and stick us in pens."

Margaret started to cry. Karen settled her on the bench with a jacket for a pillow. She fell asleep with her thumb in her mouth.

"My cousin said that some kids died of homesickness at the school." Leo jumped around to keep warm. His flannel shirt was too short in the sleeves and he wasn't wearing socks.

"How old are you?" Mary Agnes asked.

"Who cares?" Leo said. "I'm strong and smart." He made a fist.

"We could sneak off. I bet there are some caves around here, and I know how to trap and skin rabbits."

"He's thirteen," Karen said. "He has to repeat seventh grade."

Leo made a punching motion in her direction and she made one back. The moon gave just enough light to make dim shadows. Soon they were all shadow boxing except Margaret.

They walked the tracks, carefully putting one foot in front of the other. Then they raced each other, one kid on each rail—dashing to the end of the platform. Two hours later they put their hands on the rails and felt the tremor of the oncoming train.

The train pulled into the Genoa station around noon. A beat-up school bus waited. Mary Agnes felt stiff and dirty. They'd had no breakfast or place to wash and very little sleep. She felt worse than the morning after she'd had too much beer. Margaret and Karen held hands, and Leo didn't look so brave in the noon sunlight. His hair was flat in the back; his naked ankles were brown and thin.

At least I won't be alone here, she thought; I'll be with other Indians. There'll be no white kids to tease us.

The bus driver let them off at the principal's office. In rumpled clothes, Mary Agnes stood before the secretary, Mrs. Francis, according to her desk nameplate.

She looked at her papers. "Welcome, Mary Agnes. Now, I know you have an Indian name, but forget it. We only speak English here. No Indian languages are allowed."

"I'm a Crow. What's wrong with our language?"

"You must learn to live in this century. The Indian way of life is dying out. Recognize that and you'll be better off."

Mrs. Francis asked questions about her grade level and typed the answers onto a form. When finished, she ripped it out of her typewriter, and slipped it in a folder.

"There, now that's done. Here's your uniform." She handed

Mary Agnes a pile of clothes. "Put these on and give me your things."

Mary Agnes looked around. "Where's the girl's lavatory?"

"Never mind that. Just slip out of those dirty clothes—no one's likely to come in."

She laid out the new clothes on the chair, so she could dress in a hurry. A white cotton blouse and a black wool jumper. She unbuttoned her nylon blouse, shrugged it off and folded it.

"Underwear too."

Embarrassed, Mary Agnes turned her back to Mrs. Francis. She smelled sweaty and needed to wash. Hurriedly, she slipped off her old panties and stepped into the new ones. The undershirt was snug and the jumper too large.

"Good, you don't need a brassiere yet. Do you have your monthlies?"

Mary Agnes nodded.

Mrs. Francis made a note on her form. "I'll try to get you another pair of bloomers and a smaller jumper. But, I do have sixty-five students to provide for."

She came around the desk, and gave Mary Agnes's arm a small, gentle pat. "I expect you're feeling a little homesick. You'll get used to it. Give me your things, and I'll dispose of them."

Mary Agnes carefully folded her undershirt and panties inside her plaid skirt, placed her nylon blouse on top. Auntie had bought the blouse with her lease money. It cost two dollars and came in a silver box with a cellophane cover.

"Can't I keep them?" Mary Agnes was reluctant to give up her blouse. What would Auntie think if she knew?

"Best to start fresh."

Soon it was October, Mary Agnes's second month at the school. This morning, even without a watch, she knew she was late.

She hurried to class, slipping on the frosty ground and skinning her knees. Brushing the dirt off her uniform, she entered the classroom.

"Mary Agnes." Miss Grimes, the teacher, had buckteeth and a perpetual frown. When she shook her head, her curls bobbled like brown sausages on the end of a meat fork. The kids feared her. "You're late again! Hold out your hand."

Mary Agnes flinched at each stinging hit. Her hand turned red, and her palm tried to curl in on itself. Her eyes watered, and snot streaked her face.

The class was required to count the hits out loud ... eighteen, nineteen, and twenty. The last three smacks were the hardest and broke her skin. Finally, it was over and she returned to her seat. *I made it, I made it,* ran through her mind, although her hand burned and she'd leaked pee on her underpants.

She looked out the classroom window at the compound. The classroom was across from the dorms—two long low buildings with tarpaper roofs. Each housed about thirty students. The yard between was for recess. At one end of the yard was a cottonwood tree with a tire swing. That was their playground. Where would they have recess in the winter?

The laundry and the dining hall were in a small brick building adjacent to the dorms. Around the perimeter of the grounds was a barbed wire fence. No students were allowed to leave the school without permission. *What did it matter?* she thought. It's not like any of us had a place to go.

Chapter Fourteen

1942

It was laundry day at school. A cold March wind gusted. Mary
Agnes, late getting out of class, raced to the outbuilding.

Every student worked. The girls cooked, washed dishes, did
laundry and swept the dorms. The boys maintained the grounds,
kept the school vehicles running, and cleaned the classrooms. Ever
since the surprise attack on Pearl Harbor, the students did the work
of the janitor, who'd enlisted, and the cleaning woman, who left for
a factory job.

Mary Agnes pulled the wet clothes from the washer and hurried
to hang them on the clothesline. The freezing prairie wind blew
through the wet clothes. Her hands felt so stiff, she struggled to
open the clothespins.

However, her mind was on the game. Leo had challenged her to
knife-in-the-ground. He hadn't said it out loud; instead he passed
her a note in class, using the Indian name, *bechea-mapa-chewok*. She
was scared. It was a double danger, Indian language and the
forbidden game.

She fingered her knife. Pearl-handled and shiny, hidden deep in
the pocket of her jacket, it had come with her from Montana.

"Mary Agnes," Leo called. "We're over here." The group sat behind the shed. She was surprised to see two older boys, Roy and Harold, in a group of five, and that she was the only girl.

"Draw the circle," she said. "Do you all have knives?"

"Let's go." Leo drew the circle in the dirt. "Me first."

He opened his blade, balanced the knife tip on the end of his finger and flicked his wrist. The knife did a backward flip and fell outside the circle.

"Damn it," he said.

One by one, the boys threw. Three knives stuck in the circle. Now it was Mary Agnes's turn. Her hands were warmer now, and she opened the blade. It felt good in her hand, and she took a deep breath and threw. It stuck, it quivered, and glinted in the sunlight.

"Wow," one boy murmured.

Leo took another try. His knife fell flat, as did the other boys.

Mary Agnes made another stick, and another. Eventually, she'd eliminated all the boys except one.

"One more round. You can't beat Joseph Big Leggings—I'm a Flathead Indian."

Mary Agnes was shocked. She'd never heard anyone say his or her Indian name. The students without an English name sometimes used a stick to hit the list of girls and boys names on the blackboard. The name they hit became theirs. One boy hit repeatedly as the teacher told him no, no, no. He, unknowingly, was hitting the girls' list and, finally, he began to cry. Mary Agnes took his arm, pointed him to the boys' list, where he hit the name Billy.

"Lone Hill, Lone Hill," the boys chanted.

"The real version this time. I dare you." Joseph stood, his legs apart. Mary Agnes did the same. In this version, they threw the knives as close as they could to their own foot. The toss nearest was the winner. Both got really close as they threw again and again.

"Go on, Lone Hill," a boy urged. "Let's see you stick your foot."

If a player was desperate to win, they threw the knife into their own foot.

"I'll do it," she said, "if you've got a beer." A safe challenge, she figured, as no one at the school could get beer.

Roy pulled a can from under his jacket. What a surprise! Mary Agnes wondered if you could buy beer at school like you could buy gum and candy?

Roy passed it around, and Mary Agnes gulped. The foam rose in her throat like a good memory. It had been a long time, and she wanted more.

Abruptly, a shadow fell over their game. It came from the tall body of the principal.

They froze. Mary Agnes shoved her knife in her pocket, blade open. She felt it slice her thumb.

"What's the meaning of this?" Mr. Vanderweg cuffed a boy on the ear. "Give me those knives." In turn they handed over the knives, Mary Agnes last. Her left hand was shaking, and her right was bleeding.

"*No* Indian games!" He slapped Leo's shoulder. "Scrub away that circle!" He stuck his face in Roy's, and the spit flew from his mouth. "Is that beer? You'll be punished for this, all of you! Whose idea was it?"

They looked at their feet.

"I'll get it out of you. I'll find the ringleader, and you'll be sorry!"

Mary Agnes's thumb was stinging. The blood smelled like old pennies. Was she going to throw up? When would this be over?

"Did I hear someone talking Indian? Did I? Did I?" His face was red and contorted. He looked about to burst.

"Yes."

"Yes, what?"

"I used my Indian name," Joseph Big-Leggings whispered.

"You stupid, *stupid* Indians."

They waited in Mrs. Francis's office. The students sat together, heads down, hands clasped between their knees, muttering to each other.

"It's your fault, Leo, and yours too, Roy. You shouldn't have brought the beer. Boy, you're going to get it now," Joseph said.

Mary Agnes sat on the end of the bench and wouldn't look at the boys. She licked her dry, chapped lips. Her tongue was sticking to her teeth. She was desperate for a piece of gum, and rifled her pockets. The wall clock ticked away the minutes. Each tick was as loud as a slap. Mary Agnes wanted to be home. Was she going to lose her knife?

One by one, the boys were called in, coming out with their heads down. Leo whispered, "Detention, three weeks, no basketball."

Mr. Vanderweg called Mary Agnes last.

"Sit down." He opened her folder and studied the pages. "Mary Agnes?" He looked over his glasses.

She bit her lip. Thoughts of her friends filled her mind. Basketball practice would be starting soon. Would Wanda be playing forward?

He cleared his throat. "What do you have to say for yourself?"

"Why can't we play our game? It's only Mumblety-Peg."

"Why are you at school, girl? Can you tell me that?"

She felt confused. What was she supposed to say? He knew none of the students had a choice, they'd been ordered to school.

"Here's the reason, Missy. You need to forget your savage Indian ways. They won't help you now. You're here to learn how to live in a white world."

"And furthermore," he came around his desk, "you must cut off your braids." He stroked one braid and laid it down her chest.

Mary Agnes backed out the door. She ran down the hall. Outside, she bent over, gasping for air.

Leo ran out of the dusk. "So what punishment did ya get?"

"Nothing much. He kept my knife. Gave me a lecture, and

wants me back in three days." She didn't tell him about her braids, and her fear when he touched her chest. What had she done for the principal to single her out?

"What did he do? Some of the girls say to keep away from him."

"Forget about it. It's dark, the teachers can't see us." She grabbed his hand. "Let's play Old Bear."

This was the student's favorite game. They made a line and swung back and forth to avoid the kid acting as the bear who tried to grab and bite someone. If you were the last in line, you usually got bitten, and then you were the bear. They played until it was pitch dark, and the teacher blew the whistle.

The next week, Mrs. Francis excused Mary Agnes from class and sent her to the principal's office. She didn't mind leaving, as they were doing math problems she'd learned in fourth grade. Also, she'd noticed the teachers didn't bother correcting and returning their papers.

Mr. Vanderweg closed the door behind her.

"Do you know why you're here, Missy?"

"You sent for me, only I haven't done *anything* wrong." She held her arms tight to her sides.

"Why did the BIA send you here?"

She looked out the window wishing she could fly like a hawk. No, she thought, don't say it. I'm a Crow Indian, fierce and strong, and I'm not going to forget it. He stared at her, his eyes as hard as steel.

The phone rang in the outer office. She heard voices. The principal cleared his throat and spit into his handkerchief. She pulled a loose thread from the hem of her ragged coat. The minutes ticked by. A door slammed in the corridor. Mary Agnes knew she wouldn't be released until she gave in.

"Well, girl? *Well?*"

Her shoulders sagged, and it didn't seem worth it. She'd say anything to get out of there.

"To forget Indian ways," she whispered, "that's why I'm here. To learn to live in a white man's world."

"Very good." He patted her shoulder.

"Can you say that to the other students? We're having an assembly Thursday, and I want you to give a little speech."

She shook her head.

"Oh, it will be okay. I'll write it out for you. You can read it before the regular program."

She picked at her fingernails, rubbing the indent on her right forefinger where she gripped her pencil. The other kids would be mad at her.

Mr. Vanderweg opened his desk drawer, and pulled out her beautiful pocket knife. He turned it over and over in his hands, enjoying its heft. "I bet you'd like this fancy knife back."

Her heart leaped.

"I know you're good with it." He smiled. "I make it my business to know what's going on here. Do as I say, and you'll get it back."

⋙⋘

It was September; Leo and Mary Agnes had been at school for over a year. An early snow had fallen, and it was twenty-three degrees. The prairie wind whipped the leaves from the cottonwood tree, pushing the tire swing back and forth. It creaked as Mary Agnes hurried to meet Leo, as usual behind the storage shed. She slipped on a patch of snow and skidded into him. He caught her in a rough hug.

"I hate this place." He waved his arm to include all the buildings and grounds.

She blew on her hands. "Me, too."

"I'm always hungry. There were maggots in the breakfast mush, and Joseph puked all over our table. We had to finish eating before they let him clean up." He held his nose. "It stunk!"

"You can have my bread at supper. I gave it to Margaret yesterday 'cause she said her belly ached." Mary Agnes didn't mention that her stomach hurt, too.

Leo pulled his collar up to his ears. "Why are they so mean to us? We haven't done anything wrong!"

Mary Agnes cupped her hands over his ears. "They're freezing. Where's your hat?"

"I left it in the classroom." He picked up a rock and hurled it at the shed roof. It rolled down and fell to earth with a thump.

Mary Agnes remembered how Karen had to stand outside in the cold all morning after she wet her bed. And she remembered her unanswered letters to Auntie, describing conditions at the school.

Leo kicked the shed door several times, creating a small cloud of dirt and snow. "Let's run away."

Her eyes flashed. "Where to?"

"Home. I know folks on the rez."

"I bet Auntie would take you in."

Leo twirled and boxed his shadow. "Let's go, I'm ready!"

"Would we have a chance? It's getting awfully cold."

"We have a shot. Sneak away at night, and hide in the daytime till we're far away from the school. Then hitch or hop freights." Leo said.

"We need money. What do you think?" Mary Agnes asked. "Thirty bucks at least."

Leo jingled some change in his pocket. "I've saved up eighteen dollars, not enough, we need at least fifty to make a start. Once we get outta here, I can get a job at a filling station. Pumping gas, changing oil, doing tune-ups. They need guys 'cause everyone's fighting. My dad's somewhere in the Pacific."

"They won't hire an Indian."

"They might, I know everything about engines."

Mary Agnes looked at the darkening sky. "Snow tonight, for sure." She took Leo's hand. "We can steal from the principal. When I was in his office I saw him put money in his desk drawer."

Leo put his arm around her. "Does he bother you?"

She turned away, remembering Vanderweg's fingers on her braid. "I got my knife back."

"You did? How?"

"I had to read the speech." Mary Agnes said. "That's *all* I had to do." This time, she thought. What will he want next?

"What you said in the assembly? About forgetting Indian ways. Was that all?" He squeezed her hand. "No one paid attention to what you read. None of us are *ever* going to forget our people."

"June and Audrey won't talk to me. They say I'm a white Indian."

One week later at eleven p.m., Mary Agnes and Leo met at the back door of the school.

"Let's go into Grimes's room and mess it up," Leo said. She had hit him, too. "Break her chalk and flip her desk upside down." He snorted a quiet laugh.

"No, dummy. They'll know it was a student. If we take the money and don't run too soon, they can't blame us."

Leo nodded as if she could see him. "You're smart," he whispered.

Mary Agnes felt the wall along the corridor. She knew the second door with the glass panel was the principal's. "Here it is." She twisted the doorknob. "It's not locked." Leo pushed her through the door, and they paused in his outer office.

"Straight ahead is Mrs. Francis's desk." Mary Agnes moved slowly forward until she could touch it. Leo lit another match. They spotted a pair of yellow bedroom slippers peeking out from under the desk.

"Agh," Mary Agnes gasped, "for a minute I thought she was lying under her desk. The slippers must be for when her feet hurt."

Leo put his feet into the slippers and skated around the room.

Just then a light in the corridor came on. Leo froze. Mary Agnes pulled him behind the desk. They listened to the heavy footsteps in the hall. Mary Agnes held her breath and imagined a warring party of Apaches creeping toward them. She let her mind close down until she pictured herself small as a baby rabbit.

The knob turned, and the door opened. From under the desk Mary Agnes could see the janitor's boots in the doorway. He muttered under his breath something like, "Hafta check his office, hafta to check every night, he's the principal." He coughed and then backed out.

"Let's get in his office before the janitor comes back," Mary Agnes said.

They slowly opened the door to the inner office. Leo lit a match and tried to open his desk drawer. Locked. He poked the lock with his file, and it gave right away.

"There." He pulled open the drawer.

Mary Agnes lifted out and opened the cash box.

"Goddam," Leo whispered. "That's a lot of wampum." He started to scoop it into his jacket pocket.

"No." Mary Agnes pushed his hand away. "We don't take it all. That way he won't notice that some is missing."

"We need it." Leo sounded disappointed.

"We'll take some now and come back for more if he doesn't miss the first batch." She closed the drawer and stuffed some into Leo's pocket. "I'll keep some, too. Just in case someone sees us with too much money."

"Pretty smart for an Indian," Leo whispered. "Pretty damn smart."

It was late October before they made the third raid on the principal's cash box. This time they took less than twenty dollars, and their total was thirty-seven.

"Now we've got enough." Her voice quivered. "I gotta get out of here!"

"Soon," Leo said. "When the weather breaks."

Chapter Fifteen

The escape opportunity happened the second week of November after a Chinook wind. The warm breeze increased the temperature by forty degrees in a few hours, although it could plummet just as quickly.

The school grounds were slushy when Mary Agnes and Leo met after school. "Let's go tonight. Meet me here at eleven after the bed check." He stamped his feet with excitement. "Don't bring more than you can carry."

Mary Agnes packed a few things in her pillowcase, and stashed it beneath her cot. She slipped into bed wearing her clothes with her winter coat under her pillow.

The dorm was quiet. The last whispering girl fell asleep. From the next bed puffed a gentle snore. She pulled the blanket around her neck. This could be her last night at the school. Were they really going on the road? Leo had studied a map and picked out a route, and she had faith in him. She liked being with him; guess he was her boyfriend. What would Wanda think? She giggled to herself—a real boyfriend.

Her feet were cold and her forehead damp and hot. Maybe she was getting sick. Could she still change her mind? What about the other kids, especially Karen and Margaret? Was it fair to leave them? With their brother gone, Vanderweg might make them pay. She thought of his hand, yellow, jagged fingernails touching her hair. She was almost glad when they hacked off her braids. She swallowed the bile rising in her throat. His touch was gone, and yes, she needed to leave. She'd be safe with Leo.

"We're free now," Leo crowed as they slogged along the ditch toward the highway. "We'll walk all night and hole up at dawn. Tomorrow, we can hop a freight."

Mary Agnes didn't feel so free. The trees on either side of the highway seemed solid and forbidding, like closed doors. Night sounds filled the air. Rustling and scratching came from the underbrush. An owl hooted, then a coyote howled.

She concentrated on moving forward. Each footstep took her farther from the school. Getting away was all that mattered. She crunched dried grass and gravel, stumbling in the dark trying to keep up with Leo. Startled, she felt something furry brush her leg.

"Agh, what's that?"

"I felt something, too. A skunk, maybe, do you smell it? It's gone now, let's go!"

She moved her pillowcase to the other arm; it was heavy. She plunked it down. "Hold on for a minute."

She checked the contents to make sure she hadn't dropped anything: Clothes, two arithmetic books, a hairbrush, her knife and a shiny compact with a mirror. Opening the compact in the dim light she saw only a ghostly image. She touched the new red barrettes sent by Auntie. Her hair was growing fast, and she could pull it back to frame her face. With the red barrettes, she looked almost pretty.

Leo peered over his shoulder and said. "I'm counting the cars that pass. Are there more than usual? So far, none look familiar. Do they know we're gone yet? It'd be just like Vanderweg to do a late night bed check."

Mary Agnes was cold. Her shoes were wet from sloshing through the puddles. Splash! She'd just hit another. "Wish I had some rubber boots."

"We can buy some if we make it to Columbus."

"How far is that?"

"About twenty-one miles if we stay on the right highway."

Just then came a crashing in the underbrush. She grabbed Leo's arm. They crouched in the ditch as a big buck soared over their heads and disappeared into the woods.

"Wow! Did you see him?" Leo stared into the dark. "He looked like the white ghost deer."

"I saw his white belly for sure. We call him the *chía áparaaxe* deer in Crow. Remember the legend?" Mary Agnes asked.

"The legend says the bridal price is one white deer hide. Maybe I'll be the warrior to find the white ghost deer, and use the hide for your wedding dress." Leo took her hand.

Mary Agnes giggled. She hoisted her bundle, and they trudged on.

They walked most of the night, propelled by hope and the fear of getting caught. When the sky faded to gray, then pink, they spotted a farm. They hurried to the barn before daylight would give them away—two school-aged Indian children, poorly dressed, alone on the road.

They crept in and climbed to the loft. They nestled in the dusty hay. Mary Agnes groaned. She tucked her cold wet feet under Leo's leg.

Leo put his arm around her. "It's okay," he said. "We'll make it."

He leaned to kiss her goodnight, and it turned into something else. The kiss moved from lips to bodies. Side by side, length-by-length, toes touching as they moved together.

Mary Agnes finally pushed him away. It took all of her strength and will power. Not being able to stop was overwhelming, frightening and surprising. She knew many unmarried Indian girls with babies. Now, she understood how it happened. The kisses didn't want to stop.

Leo put his hand under her shirt, and she pushed him away. "Enough for now," she said.

The hay prickled, stabbing her in the back and legs. Her feet finally warmed up, only her thoughts ran on and on as she listened to Leo's even breathing. What was happening at the school? She hoped the other students weren't being punished. She wished Vanderweg wouldn't bother to hunt them. Maybe he didn't care. He could lie about the number of students to the BIA. Some other unlucky Indian student could encourage them to forget the old way of life. She was tired of being the chosen one. Shifting her thoughts to basketball and the smell of fry bread in Auntie's kitchen, she finally drifted into sleep.

Mary Agnes woke to the sound of drips as the ice melted off the barn roof. Sunlight filtered through the loose boards, and she knew it was past time to go. She shook Leo, and he looked panicked. Bits of hay stuck in his hair, his eyes were wide and scared. Mary Agnes brushed the hay from his hair.

Just then a door slammed.

Leo held a finger to his lips as the barn door slid open. They clutched each other as a dog barked.

"*Bishké*," Mary Agnes whispered.

"Come on, boy, I'm in here, come on. That's a good boy, Rufus." They heard the dog panting. Leo pinched his nose to stifle a sneeze. He dislodged some hay and dust, and it floated through the floorboards. The dog barked louder.

"What is it, Rufus? Is someone up there?" The man's gravely

voice paused. "If anyone is there, you best come down now!"

Leo shook his head no, his body frozen in place.

Footsteps thudded on the ladder, then a man appeared in a sheepskin coat and cowboy hat.

"Well, what have we here?" He seemed more curious than threatened.

"Hullo," Leo said. "We're on our way to our Auntie's house. She lives in Jefferson."

"What's her name, boy?"

"Uh—" Leo looked at Mary Agnes, "we just call her Auntie. Her family name is Baker and her man is a rancher."

"Come with me."

At the back door he told them to wait. A face looked out the window.

"I don't want them Indians in the house," a woman with a whiny voice said.

"They're just kids," he said, "lost or runaways. Cain't do no harm."

He let them in the kitchen. A woman with a heavy wool sweater over her nightgown sat at the table finishing her coffee. She didn't acknowledge them.

Mary Agnes looked away from the plates smeared with egg yolk and bacon grease. Her stomach growled. What a mean woman! She must know they were hungry. She pictured the woman in her bathrobe running from a Crow warrior across the plains, then roped and dragged through the sagebrush.

The rancher lifted the receiver of the wall phone and heard the tinny women's voices on the party line.

"The damn cacklers are on." He put it to his ear. "I gotta make an important call," he growled, "so hang up, will ya?"

The woman thumped the plates in the sink. She pulled her sweater tight over her chest and shuffled out of the kitchen.

He got the line open.

"Mel? Is that you? Ya, it's melting here too. By this time next week, it'll be snowing again." He shifted the phone to his other ear, leaned his lanky frame against the wall. "Found some kids in my barn this morning. Yup, they're Indians. Know any rancher named Baker with an Indian gal?" He took a toothpick out of the holder on the table. "Me, neither. Guess I'll call that Indian School in Genoa. You got the number? Thanks, see you at the Grange on Tuesday."

He pointed an accusing finger to the kids. Mary Agnes hung her head; her black hair curtained her eyes. She felt helpless.

Leo swallowed. "Mister, can't you let us go? We're making no trouble, and we'll be down the road before you know it. They treat us something terrible at the Indian School. We eat rotten food and get beatings, and we're trying to get home."

The rancher moved his toothpick to the other side of his mouth.

"We'll do chores for you. I can fix any kind of machine and my friend, Mary Agnes, can clean. Can you give us a chance?"

"I'm a good worker," Mary Agnes begged. "I'll clean all day for a plate of food. I can bake, too."

"You can't do that," the woman called from the other room. "Them's runaways."

"That's right," He pulled his hat low on his forehead. "Got to turn you in. Don't want you stealing our eggs or scaring our stock."

Afraid, hungry and tired, Leo and Mary Agnes waited on the back steps. Mary Agnes felt cold despite the sun on her face. Her thoughts scurried like ants in spilled sugar. What to do, how could they get away? She knew they were in for a bad time. She grabbed Leo's arm. "Let's hide in the woods. We have an hour before they get here."

"Naw." Leo shrugged. "That'll just make it harder on us when we do get caught. Let's go back to the school, take our punishment, and run away in the spring."

The truck pulled up and the driver yelled at them. "Get in, Mr. Vanderweg is waiting. You're dead meat!"

"Mr. Nelson, can we ride up front? It's cold."

"Get in back!"

The sun was out, the wind had picked up, and it was no Chinook. They huddled together, their backs against the cab. They didn't feel hungry or cold, only worried.

"What's going to happen?" Mary Agnes whispered, the wind whipping her hair from her face.

"What more can they do?"

"They can do plenty!"

"It'll just be a beating and maybe more chores."

"I can take a beating, only he can do things to me he wouldn't do to you." She remembered Mr. Vanderweg's hand on her braid, and she slid to the edge of the truck bed.

"Like what?" Leo asked.

"You're so stupid! He could force me like he did the other girls." She inched closer.

He grabbed her jacket. "No, no! Don't jump."

"I can't go back!"

"It's not worth jumping, you'll get hurt. I'll say it was my fault— I *made* you go!"

"It won't work. He hates us, they all hate us 'cause we're Indians."

"Not Mrs. Francis, not Ida—I'll talk to them."

"Can we try again?"

"Yes." He pulled her close to the cab. "We'll wait for things to calm down. Bide our time. Act real sorry and then we'll go in the spring. Can you last till then?"

"Maybe. What about the money? How can we keep the money?"

"I hid it in the lining of my shoe."

"Give me some. I'll hide it in my jacket. Promise me we'll run away soon."

"I promise," he whispered.

Mary Agnes bent her head as tears streaked her cheeks. She turned from Leo, covered her face with her hands and sobbed. He pulled his cap over his eyes. He didn't want her to see *his* tears.

Chapter Sixteen

The truck sped back. They looked for the white deer, although the previous night now felt like a dream. The distance they'd trudged turned into a little more than two hours in the truck. As Mr. Nelson stopped at the classroom building, the sun was out and the playground was empty. The only signs of life were the faces in the classroom windows.

The principal waited on the front steps. He dragged them to the assembly hall where he had rounded up the teachers and the students.

The hall was quiet. He walked back and forth a few times, his hands clasped behind his back.

"Students," he began, "we have a problem. These two Indians stole my money and ran away. They need to be punished. Any ideas?"

The students were silent. The escapees were their friends. What should they say? They looked at each other and the teachers. No one wanted to speak.

"If you don't help, I'll assume you were in on it and you'll be punished, too."

Finally, Billy raised his hand.

"Go on, Billy, what's your idea?"

"Hit'em with the ruler, make 'em clean toilets."

"Anyone else?" His eyes fired at the students. "You stand to gain if you have good ideas. Here are two students that ran off and caused the school to be shut down. How do we teach them a lesson?"

Joseph waved his arm. "Take away their good stuff, like knives, slingshots and marbles."

"Good, come and help me."

He took the bundles from Mary Agnes and Leo, and dumped them on the floor.

"Okay, Joseph, hold these things up, one by one. Students, pick what you want from these thieves and runaways."

First, he held up Mary Agnes's clothes. The students kept quiet. Finally, Karen waved her arm. Next, the math teacher claimed her textbooks, and Billy took Leo's clothes.

"Joseph, describe this pouch." Vanderweg thumped him on the head with his ruler.

He looked in the leather pouch. "Some steelies and cat eye marbles."

Several boys waved their hands. Leo flinched. He'd worked hard to win the marbles, especially his steelies. They went from tiny to a half-inch in diameter. Finally, he tossed the bag to Harold.

The giveaway went on. Mary Agnes gasped when he held up her compact.

"This is a girl's thing. I don't know what to call it," Joseph said.

The principal opened it, looked in the mirror, and patted his thinning ginger-colored hair.

"Appears to be a small powder box with a mirror. Very nice!"

The girls were quiet. They all wanted the compact, only they wouldn't take it from Mary Agnes. They remembered when Auntie sent it to her. The principal held it in the air.

"I'll smash it if no one claims it."

Finally, Margaret raised her arm. Joseph delivered it to her small, waiting hand.

Next, Joseph reached deep in the pillowcase to pull out the hairbrush and toothbrush. Vanderweg grunted, "Those are dirty, dirty things," and threw them in the trashcan. Last, Joseph brought out the red barrettes.

Mary Agnes held out her hand. "I need those for my hair, which you made me cut."

Vanderweg slapped her hand away. "Too late!" He pocketed them.

In an instant, she knew the answer to her problem. It wasn't enough to run away from the school. No, something worse had to happen to their tormentor. She remembered pictures of warriors with scalps on their lances—bloody scalps. Coyote could trick the principal, and she'd be ready with her blade. She concentrated on the image: His patch of hair pasted by blood to her knife. Kill, *dappee*!

Joseph held up the last item. Mary Agnes's knife.

Everyone was quiet. They knew it was her prize possession, and that Mary Agnes was the best in the school at *bechea-mapa-chewok*. No one raised a hand; they could see the pain on her face.

"Tell you what, students, I'm going to keep this. The pupil with the highest grade average at the end of the school year will win this prize." He held the knife in the air. Opened and closed it—click, click.

Mary Agnes held on to her image. Vanderweg scalped with her knife. How she would never clean her knife again. And how she could watch his head bleed into the dirt until his skinny legs gave one last twitch.

"Billy," he paused, "you start the whipping. Mary Agnes and Leo, bare your legs, and lean over the chairs." He handed a paddle, long and sturdy, to Billy. Leo pulled down his pants and Mary Agnes lifted the back of her jumper.

"Billy, hit both, then pass the paddle. Everyone strikes once. Make it hard! I'm watching!"

Swack, swack. Billy hit Leo, then Mary Agnes.

Swack, swack. Their bodies jerked and absorbed the hits.

Billy was small, so he didn't hit too hard. The next students were bigger and stronger.

The principal urged them on. "I'm watching you, remember, they're runaways, and I want my money back!"

The beating went on. By now, thirty of the sixty students had wielded the paddle. The skin on their legs was flayed. Neither Leo nor Mary Agnes had made a sound. Mary Agnes's nose ran, although she wouldn't cry. She imagined striking Vanderweg on *his* legs, hands, and ears.

Leo groaned as the paddle struck.

Mary Agnes sent Leo some power—I'm Crow, you're Blackfeet, take back our land. She pictured herself on a mountain, surrounded by lances with powerful medicine feathers.

As ten more students struck him, Leo slumped to the floor.

Vanderweg grabbed the paddle. Slap, slap, slap, it seemed to go on forever.

Leo cried out, "Stop, please, stop." He got up and fell again. "I'll give you the money! I can't take it anymore!"

Vanderweg gave the paddle to the last student. "Hit 'em hard, you're the last," he crowed.

Finally, it ended.

Mary Agnes crouched on the floor, her face impassive as stone, her mind far away. Her jumper stuck to her bloody legs, and she wouldn't rub them or acknowledge her wounds.

Leo held his arms over his face and wept. He was broken.

"I want my money!" the principal screamed.

Leo pulled off his bloody shoe. With a shaking hand, he peeled back the lining and revealed the wrinkled bills.

"Back to the dorms! Now! There'll be no more runaways!"

The girls whispered to each other as the matron arrived in the dorm, herding Mary Agnes. The matron wore a black dress, her hair pulled back so tightly it nearly stretched her eyes to her ears. Her mouth was pursed in a tight line. Everything about her was rigid, even her voice, "Here's some salve," she squeezed the words from her thin lips. "Put it on your wounds."

The girls crowded around Mary Agnes. "Does it hurt? Let me see. Ugh!"

One girl gave her a shove. "You got us all in trouble. They tore up our cots, made us stay in, questioned us."

"Well, you took my stuff!" She turned to look at her legs. Bloody stripes like candy canes covered the backs.

"Sorry," Karen said. "You can have your clothes back."

"Your compact, too." Margaret handed it to her. "I took it so I could give it back to you."

Mary Agnes polished the compact with the hem of her jacket. "Thank you, thanks. Sorry, I'm sorry, everyone. I didn't want to hurt you, only I *had* to go!" She hunched her shoulders and sobbed.

Betty, one of the older girls, put her arm around Mary Agnes. "I know what you mean. I used to be his favorite before you came."

"I'm not his favorite! I just had to cooperate."

"Did he hurt you?"

"No, not yet. He held onto my knife until I gave a speech, which you all heard. He stares at me and follows me around."

"He picked on you till you gave in, like he did me," Betty said. "He's evil. I'm going to talk to Mrs. Francis or the matron."

"Don't! Anything you say will only make it worse for me."

Mary Agnes felt cold as she sat by the river. Hours had passed while she recalled her early life. The sun was down and the evening star glowed high and bright as she had one last thought—things did get worse for her at school.

She shivered and shook off the past.

For supper she'd open a can of beans and then go to bed. Tomorrow, she needed to be at Henderson's early. Toilets to clean, sheets to change, pots and pans to scrub, napkins and tablecloths to iron. Maybe, she'd have time to put Harry on the Hi-Fi.

She rubbed her tired back and went inside.

Chapter Seventeen

1958

Patsy yawned so loud, her jaw creaked. Last night another hang-up phone call had disturbed her, and at the back of her mind lurked that *goddamn loan payment.*

Where was Coach this early morning, his muscled arms and quiet hands?

Had the word gotten around about the Indian haircut she'd done? Sleep wasn't possible, so she dressed. Too early for work, she steered her Oldsmobile to the Johnny Café, enjoying the empty streets, the gray and pink dawn.

"Coffee," she ordered. The place was empty except for a man reading the newspaper in a booth, quiet except for the clanking of dishes in the kitchen. A waitress in a hair net and nylon uniform swept the worn linoleum floor. Patsy blew on her coffee and took a cautious sip.

A car pulled up in front. Surprisingly, she spotted Coach's tan arm as he pushed open the door. He took the seat next to her. She quickly ran her tongue over her front teeth to remove any lipstick and straightened her slouched back.

"Morning," she ventured.

He turned to her. You could pack for a week in his eye bags.

There was a small patch of stubble his razor had missed, like a line of dirt along his jaw.

"Morning," he answered." What are you doing out so early?"

"I couldn't sleep."

"Same here."

"Is anything wrong?" Patsy surprised herself by asking.

"Christ!" He slammed his coffee cup into the saucer.

Patsy jumped.

"Damn it to hell, why would she do that to me and the kids? I know I'm gone a lot, except it's all work, damn hard work!"

Patsy nodded, not knowing what to say. She began to put things together. Bobbi wasn't the only problem. The last time she'd done Lois's hair, she'd observed the secret glow of a woman feeling desired, maybe long neglected, now sought after. Who was it? Another teacher, or the banker with the Fred Astaire mustache? Patsy had spotted the banker's intentions. She was used to married men hitting on her.

"Come over to the shop, and we can talk."

Why *had* she invited him? Today, she had no defenses against this man. If he'd been cocky and sure of himself, she could flirt and then turn him down. Instead, he resembled a wounded cocker spaniel with sad brown eyes and silent whimpers.

Patsy closed the shop door behind them. She filled a glass with cold water and took a little sip, as if the water was the danger and not her attraction. Coach sat in the wicker chair. He didn't seem to know what to do with his hands. They ended up resting on his knees.

She straightened the magazines. "Is it Bobbi?"

"I should get to work. What time is it, anyway?"

"Only seven-thirty." Patsy said. "By the way, Bobbi's doing a good job. She's a sharp kid."

"Think so?" Coach ran his hand through his hair. "She's sneaking around doing something, God knows what. I'm sure you don't want to hear *my* problems."

"Got to talk to someone—might as well be me. Are things okay at home? She seems upset with her mom and mentioned driving a convertible."

"That's Miss Bauer's car. She's been spending too much time with her students, acting strange. I *forbade* Bobbi to see her! In fact, I'm going to the school board. Then there's a boy, I can almost hear her swooning," Coach said.

"Typical teen," Patsy replied.

Coach rubbed his bristly jaw.

She touched his arm. "Do you want me to talk to Bobbi? I can relate. I had plenty of trouble at her age."

"Yeah. I'd appreciate that. Gotta go," he muttered. "Thanks."

Patsy shivered with a premonition. Unhappy mother, angry father, Bobbi could be in serious trouble.

Patsy had told no one about her own early pregnancy. Maybe sharing with Bobbi would help the teen avoid heartbreak. Could she head her off at the pass?

When Bobbi showed up, Patsy sat her in the styling chair.

"Are you in the mood for a talk? I'll make it short, I promise."

"Am I getting a lecture?" Bobbi checked her reflection in the mirror. "What about the cleaning?"

"That can wait. I don't know what's going on with you. You've mentioned that things at home aren't that good."

Bobbi yawned. "Nothing's going on."

"Don't give me that bullshit!"

"You couldn't even make a guess, it's *so* bad!"

"Try me."

After a long minute, Bobbi said. "My mom's been sneaking out at night." She didn't mention the Indian bar or when she saw her mom making out in a stranger's car.

"My mom and dad drank every night at Stockman's Bar, while I waited in the car with my little sisters," Patsy said.

"Gross!" Bobbi said.

"It was scary. A crazy man would stand by the car and stare at us."

"How old were you?"

"Seven. My sisters were five and three. Then, when I was ten, a man at the bar tried to kiss me. After that I stayed home and did the cooking, cleaning, and watching my sisters."

"I don't get it. Where were your lovely parents?"

"During the day my dad was a cook at the café and mom waited tables. Like I said, they drank every night."

"So, what's your point?"

Patsy shook her head. "Like you, I was unhappy at home. I learned secretarial skills so I could get a job and leave. However, my plans were destroyed in a minute, and I don't want that to happen to you."

"Does that mean you got pregnant or something—had to get married?" Bobbi asked. She wondered why Patsy was talking to her about this personal stuff?

"Yes. If the baby had lived, she'd be about your age."

"That's sad." Bobbi picked hairs from a comb. "I saw a dead baby at the mortuary. The coffin was too long like they expected she was going to grow into it or something."

Patsy turned her back as tears stung her eyes. She was surprised by her emotion. "Well, it's ancient history. Don't worry about it."

"Anyone can see that you're about to cry."

Patsy blew her nose. "Sorry, I didn't mean to make this about me. Mainly, I'm worried about you."

Bobbi gave a slight smile. "I do have a serious crush on a guy. He hasn't asked me out yet, so I don't see how I could get pregnant."

"The Indian ball player, Mary Agnes's son?"

"He's so cute!" Bobbi spun the chair around. "I'd do anything to get a date with him!"

Patsy lit a cigarette and blew out the match. "Do girls in your school date Indians?"

Bobbi ran her fingers along the teeth of the comb, making a scratching sound. "If he's good enough to play on the team, he's good enough to date! I'm going to give him a ride in a convertible."

"The teacher's car? I've heard some things. You don't want your reputation ruined by her, either."

"It isn't just me. We all want to drive her car."

Patsy patted her back, surprised at the teen's sharp shoulder blades. "Listen, Bobbi, I don't want to preach. I'm here to listen. Just don't do *anything* rash."

Bobbi sat quietly. Jeez, she wished her mom *had* asked what was going on, and offered to listen for once. She wished that she hadn't seen her mom sneaking out, that Rita and Donna were still her friends, and that she could decide about going overnight with Jean. Maybe, she *should* talk to Patsy.

However, just then Patsy waved her off. "I don't have time for more talking right now. I have a shop to run."

Chapter Eighteen

P atsy drove fast. Mag and Lois, as they asked her to call them, had invited her to the steak fry at the lake. She was supposed to meet Gordon, the new single band teacher. A new guy. Would he be as handsome as Coach? How would he measure up to her ex-husband, Ordell?

Lately, she'd been missing Ord more and more. The group at the lake would all be couples. She missed being married and saying, "I'll check with my hubby and let you know," when activities came around.

She'd met Ord at Ruth's Salon when he came to do electrical work. Tall as a well-watered hollyhock, his gray eyes drew her in. Long sweeping lashes showcased an expression of pure kindness. She could absolutely trust this man. And his flannel shirts in soft colors made her want to stroke his back. They'd started dating just as her divorce from Ronnie was final. Recently, he'd helped Patsy move to her new place.

"What can I do for Ord?" she asked Ruth. "He's been taking me out to eat most nights."

"That's easy," Ruth said. "Invite him to your place for supper. There's nothing like the smell of a pot roast. It makes men swoon."

"It's the same with pie." The lady under the dryer lifted the hood. "An apple pie will bring them to their knees."

Patsy said. "I've never made pie crust or a roast."

Ruth groaned. "Both easy. I'll give you my grandmother's secret pie crust recipe."

Patsy looked at the dough. The results of the secret pie crust recipe, including a teaspoon of vinegar, were in the garbage

For her second attempt, she'd consulted the open page in her *Betty Crocker Cookbook.*

The dough kept breaking apart, and she finally rolled it large enough to cover the pie plate. She transferred it gingerly. Then she mended the parts where it separated. Finally, she added apples and sugar, and set it in the oven. In no way did it resemble the pie in the picture.

"Hi," she greeted Ord as he climbed the stairs. He held out a small bunch of daisies.

"Thank you." She went into the kitchen to get a mason jar for the flowers. He followed her. "What do I smell cooking?"

"Pot roast. It's not done yet."

"Give me a look around," Ord said. "When I carried in your things, I didn't see everything."

She showed him the bathroom and the large closet.

"Wow, that's huge." Ord stepped in, pulled Patsy closer and put his arms around her. "It's big enough for a baby crib."

She pushed him away and thought, there might be a baby in that closet, except it won't be mine. After losing the baby with Ronnie, she'd vowed not to put herself through another failure.

The roast never did get tender, the gravy was thin, and the pie crust was too brown. Ord and Patsy ate every bite, pretending it was delicious.

After they had done the dishes, the two sat on the couch. Ord put his arm around her and tilted her chin up for a kiss. Patsy kissed him back. His lips weren't dry and chapped like Ronnie's. Eventually, his lips worked their way around to the back of her neck then gradually down to her breasts. She felt tingly all over.

When Ord slipped his hand between her legs, she removed her skirt so it wouldn't get wrinkled.

"How does this thing work?" Ord started to unfold the convertible couch.

"Like this." She pulled out the frame and mattress and hooked the two sections together.

Ord gently pushed her down. He unhooked her bra and opened her blouse. Then he kissed her stomach for a long time. Patsy felt like she was melting, like her legs would flow right off the bed. When he got up to remove his own clothes, she closed her eyes. She'd never actually seen Ronnie's thing, and she didn't want to see Ord's, either. However, when Ord stretched beside her, she'd never felt so tense and excited. The parts that had melted snapped back into place like they'd been whipped.

He pulled her to him and they touched everywhere—lips, chest, stomach, knees and toes. Unlike Ronnie's plump, immature body, Ord was all muscle and sinew. His bony knees scraped hers and when she ran her toe along his shin, it felt sharp enough to cut.

I'm just going to die, she thought as she clutched him. He pulled her on top of him, something Ronnie had never done. It felt right as he placed himself inside her. She moved in a new way. Back and forth, back and forth, first slow, then faster until she went one way and the bed another. It was like a confluence of heavenly bodies, except not the sun, moon, stars and planets—it was pelvis, hips, stomachs and legs.

Abruptly, the two parts of the sofa bed came unhooked and

caused his pelvis to slam hers in just the right place. She held tight and rode him down, down, down between the sections of the bed until a roman candle shot through her body and exploded in long sweet trails of orange sparks. Her first.

Who would ever measure up to Ord? She missed him like crazy. She missed the sex, the friendship, and their whole life together. The screw up was hers, because she couldn't handle another pregnancy. Why hadn't she told him how she felt? Instead, she'd made the horrible mistake that sank their marriage.

Chapter Nineteen

1958

Fort Peck Lake came into Patsy's view—steel gray waves and the rocky shore. A lone boat roiled the waters, leaving a fifty-foot wake.

The screened-in-patio was perched on a hill overlooking the lake. The aroma of sage rose up as she parked.

Inside, the gathering seemed warm and cold. Huge half-frozen steaks rested on the counter, one lapping over and dripping blood on the concrete floor. The men grouped in the main room with the picnic tables. Friendly women's voices rose from the kitchen, so she headed their way.

"Isn't this the cutest?" Mag held out her purse. "Look at the cherries." The admiring women scrutinized her handbag, which was a white plastic box with red fruit crowning the top.

"Oh, hi, Patsy," Lois said.

Patsy could feel their eyes on her. She was glad that she had chosen a plain polished cotton sundress with a cardigan, pink, of course. Her jewelry was understated, only a silver ankle bracelet engraved with her name. She wanted to be just a little bit sexy and a little more modest. After all, she didn't want to compete with these ladies; she desperately needed them for customers.

Mag took her arm and steered her to her date, the one single man in the place. They were strays meant for each other. She wondered why married women were working so hard to bring her into their fold. Did they love scouring toilets, frying chops, starching shirts so much that they wanted her to have the opportunity? Or did they want to keep her away from *their* husbands?

Gordon was not attractive. He was chubby, wore horn-rimmed glasses and had hands as big as baseball mitts. He stood a little closer to her than necessary. Patsy had to fight the impulse to pull back.

"I'm new in town, too. I teach band and Spanish," he said.

"What an interesting combo," Patsy fibbed. She found nothing attractive about this big man. On the other hand, Coach, his starched white shirt rolled back to display tanned forearms, was the best-looking guy in the room. Patsy glanced his way and caught him staring at her.

"What do you think?" Mag asked later as the women cleaned up in the kitchen. They'd finished a huge meal of steak, baked potatoes, salad and rhubarb pie.

"Nice," Patsy replied.

"*Nice?* He's single and comes from a good family in Minnesota. His father was president of the bank. No brothers or sisters, only an elderly mother."

"Quite nice," Patsy said.

Everyone laughed.

In the main room someone plugged in the record player. The first record that dropped was a foxtrot. Gordon held out his hand. Patsy followed his lead. Quite a dancer, she thought, he was light on his feet in a way that big men frequently are. They danced and danced. Gordon was sweating with the effort. Patsy pretended not to see his loose white shirt displaying a patch of pink belly with a mat of black hair.

As they rested on the sidelines for a minute, Coach came over. "Let me borrow your date?"

"Of course." Gordon wiped his brow. "I need a break; she's wearing me out."

Patsy stood on tiptoe to place her hand on Coach's neck. He pulled her close, his hand on the small of her back. She smelled the starch in his shirt and his aftershave. Her calves felt tense; her body was one long tight muscle.

"What do you think of our little get-together?" Coach whirled her to a corner of the room, and she felt the swish of her skirt on her bare legs.

"The lake is beautiful. Did you notice the sky?"

"The sky? No, I noticed you tiptoeing to the door."

Patsy laughed. "That was so my heels wouldn't sink into the gravel."

He dipped her low. She felt secure and let her head drop close to the floor. Then once more around the room, and it was over.

"Thanks." He returned her to Gordon.

The rest of the evening was a blur. Someone opened a bottle of Canadian Club and filled small paper cups. Everyone drank and danced until after midnight. Gordon walked her to her car.

"Nice meeting you."

"Thanks. Great to meet you, too."

She knew he would call by the way he leaned in the car window to say goodnight. Of course, he would call, and she'd probably go out with him.

On the ride home she rolled down the windows and turned up the radio. The night air lay on her neck like a silk scarf. For once, she remembered all the words to the familiar music, and sang along.

Once home she sat in the backyard, her bare toes curled in the grass. She'd picked up a small round stone from the driveway and ran it over her lips.

The dance with Coach had turned her on—attraction like she'd felt before. Except now she wouldn't act. She liked Bobbi a lot, and she needed Lois's business. Men like Coach could be dangerous.

Chapter Twenty

Mrs. Henderson was on the phone when Mary Agnes arrived. She put her hand over the receiver. "You can start on the beds," she said. "By the way, your hair looks better."

Mary Agnes nodded. She was light-headed from the beers she'd had last night, and she steadied herself against the wall. When Mrs. Henderson mentioned Pretty Weasel, she crept closer.

"Lois, you better do it." Mrs. Henderson said. Except, it wasn't do it, Mary Agnes decided, it was cool it. Shocked, she heard the words again in her mind. "Lois, there's talk about you and the ball player. For now, you'd better cool it."

Mary Agnes raced to the bedrooms, her heart pounding. Now it made sense. She'd heard that a town woman was sneaking around with the new basketball player. Was it Mrs. Vernon, and how was Mrs. Henderson involved? Maybe it was just gossip. What white woman would be so stupid?

Dammit, she needed to warn her son! It was Friday; she could find him at practice.

Mary Agnes went about her chores faster than usual. She made the beds, without putting on clean sheets, figuring the kids would never notice. After Mrs. Henderson left, she only vacuumed the traffic areas. She worked as fast as a hummingbird, not even putting a record on the hi-fi or doing her usual dance steps. What to do, what to do? Who could she talk to?

Unexpectedly, Mrs. Henderson touched her shoulder. Mary Agnes jumped a foot.

"Sorry, I came back to ask you something."

"Yes, ma'am." Mary Agnes caught her breath.

"How is your son?" Mrs. Henderson's voice faltered a little. "Do you see him?"

"What do you want with him? He's just an Indian boy trying to get by."

"Oh, come on, he's more than getting by, he is our star player! I have a friend that needs to contact him. Can you get him this message?" Mrs. Henderson wrote something on notepaper and sealed it in an envelope.

"Thank you, Mary Agnes." Mrs. Henderson put her hand on her arm. "It's about time I gave you a raise."

Mary Agnes jammed the note in her pocket. She needed to find Pretty Weasel now!

Chapter Twenty-One

Bobbi hesitated at Patsy's door. It was Friday at four, her usual time to start work, except she felt nervous. Setting up the fake youth church retreat, so she could go overnight to the basketball game with Jean, had been too easy.

Her mom hadn't asked all the annoying questions. *Where are you going? What time will you be home? And who is going with you?* It was as if she was someone else's child.

Everything felt weird today. Her stomach felt heavy, about to fall between her knees. She wanted so much to go to Williston and drive that bitchin' car, except she'd just die if she got found out.

"Here," Patsy pointed to the sink, which was full of hairbrushes and combs. "Wash and sort them. You know where they go."

Bobbi hurriedly rinsed them, accidently dropping the sink sprayer on the counter so it whipped around like a striking snake. Water spurted everywhere. The ladies under the dryers held up their magazines as shields, and squealed as if they'd seen a mouse. Patsy grabbed the sprayer and pinched it off. Bobbi wiped the counter, the wall and the floor. She mumbled "sorry" and continued drying the combs.

Next, Bobbi wiped the bathroom fixtures, and swept the hair from under the styling chair.

"What's your rush? You're flying around like a *bat out of hell,*" Patsy said. "Sit down. You're making me dizzy!"

"Can't." She emptied the trash and grabbed the tissues that fell on the floor.

"What's going on with you, anyway? Is it your friends again?" Patsy asked.

"Yeah, well, what friends? I feel like running away."

Bobbi wished she could ask Rita or Donna or even Patsy about the overnight trip with Jean. She dropped each clean comb into the plastic box with a snap like she was punishing them for being bright and sparkly. "I *hate* my parents, especially my mother! You should have heard them fighting last night. Cripes, I had to plug my ears."

Was the fight about her? Patsy wondered. Had someone at the steak fry noticed her chemistry with Coach? Or seen him at her shop? Adding to Bobbi's troubles was the last thing she wanted to do. "You told me about your mom sneaking out at night, anything new on that?"

Bobbi rolled her eyes. "She's wearing gobs of perfume and low-neck blouses. I swear her tits were going to fall out!" Bobbi's voice broke. "I can't say any more."

"You poor kid!" Patsy gave her a tight hug. "How can I help?"

Bobbi shook off her tears. "I just want to get away from here! Can you imagine me in Miss Bauer's convertible?"

Patsy put her hands on her hips. "Right now, I don't have time to imagine anything. I've got a special going on perms, and I have to pack in the heads. Can I count on you to work tomorrow? Did I mention I have a *loan* coming due?"

"I'm going to a church retreat, and I won't be back until late Saturday."

"Do you have to go?"

Bobbi was tempted to say more, as Patsy looked concerned.

How could she explain what was going on? How she felt she must go to Williston. If she didn't, Rita or Donna or both would go, and she would miss her chance to drive.

She didn't want to talk or even think about what her mom was doing, *who* she was meeting. No one, not even Patsy, would understand.

Bobbi worked a few more minutes, straightening the magazines, and emptying the ashtrays. Patsy slipped to the back of the trailer, and looked up the Vernons' phone number. Would Lois think she was out of line? No matter, someone had to head off Bobbi. She seemed to be spinning out of control. The phone rang and rang. Where was Bobbi's mother? She vowed to try again later.

"If you change your mind, I'll pay you double for tomorrow," Patsy said as she returned to the shop.

Bobbi shrugged and left, nearly falling over Mary Agnes, who sat on the doorstep. She motioned Bobbi to the back of the trailer. "Here, you want a beer?"

Bobbi took a sip of the warm beer. "What's up? I have to go in a minute."

"Something's going on with my boy." Mary Agnes plunged her hands into her pockets. "He won't talk to me. Can you try?"

"*Me?*" Bobbi squeaked. "You're his mom."

"He's going to be in bad trouble," Mary Agnes whispered. "Indians can play ball, but they can't mix with the whites."

Bobbi cracked her gum. "This is 1958. No one cares anymore. You even said that he might date me. He's on the team, and the white kids think he's cool."

Mary Agnes shook her head. "This is different. This woman is well-known, older and married!" She belched. "I have a note for him from Mrs. Henderson."

"Let me see it," Bobbi commanded.

Mary Agnes took the note from her pocket. "See, it says Pretty Weasel. It's not for you."

Bobbi grabbed the envelope and held it up to the light. "Maybe I can read it through the paper."

"Stay out of this!"

"I need to know what's going on," Bobbi said. "Let's go to the streetlight." She tore it open and read:

Meet L tomorrow night at 10 pm behind the Montana. Trouble.

It was quiet except for a car on the highway. The moths circled and pinged against the streetlight. Bobbi's mouth felt as dry as sand. She needed a Chiclet or a wad of bubble gum. She mouthed the message again as Mary Agnes shuffled away. What did it mean?

Bobbi waited by the gym door as the players came out. Each wore the topcoat that Coach insisted on, and their crew cuts were damp from the showers. The pain in her middle almost doubled her over. What now? Didn't she have enough to worry about?

She gestured when she saw Pretty Weasel. "Psst. Over here." He followed her to the back of the building.

Bobbi could hardly stand it. Her heart pounded, and her hand shook. "I have something for you."

"You're Coach's girl. What's your name again?"

"Bobbi."

"That's right." Pretty Weasel ran his hand over his hair. "What's up?"

Bobbi was stunned. She'd thought about him so much, and he wasn't even sure of her name! God, all those times she'd listened to *Red Sails in the Sunset,* while hugging herself and seeing Pretty Weasel coming to her from across the lake. What about her dreams of dancing in the gym, wearing his class ring, snuggling in his car?

No dream. He stood here with smooth brown skin, a black brush of hair, dark clear eyes, and brows like wings. The boy-smell of clean sweat and Brylcreem made her knees weak. He was real, and close enough to kiss.

"So, what's the deal?" he asked.

All at once it hit her. She put two and two together—a weight dropped on her chest. She couldn't breathe! The black shapes in the Buick. It was *her mother* and Pretty Weasel! Could it be? Yes, it had been his car in their driveway. She could see it in her mind's eye. Vomit rose in her throat. She thrust the paper at his chest and whirled to leave.

"Hey, what's this?" He grabbed her shoulder and she felt the strength of his hand.

"It's for you," she spit the words. "A meeting."

"What?" He frowned. "Who am I supposed to meet?"

"Your girlfriend, *my mother*, but your girlfriend!"

He stared at the note as Bobbi stomped away. What the hell? Who wrote it? Jeez, he'd kinda forgotten about Bobbi. Somehow, she knew her mom was seeing him—a teen and an Indian! No wonder she was upset.

The note said *trouble;* a lot of things could be trouble. If it involved Lois, it could be bad. He'd had a little fun with her, that's for sure, over the two months they'd been meeting. Initially, he just wanted a boost up to the team. He needed all the help he could get—an Indian with a few Ds on his report card.

However, at some point he began to desire her more and more, and she, the Coach's wife, wanted to be with him. It was flattering and hard to believe. She was young, giggly and so sexy when they were together. She had a kind of need he shared—to be wanted, to be recognized. Like the feeling he craved from basketball.

Pretty Weasel remembered the last time he and Lois had met a week ago. He'd parked on the levee behind the Civic Center, and cracked the window. Only a few mosquitoes buzzed his head, not nearly as bad as in summer. His fingers drummed on the steering wheel with impatience. Where was she?

The river trickled behind him and an owl screeched in the trees. It was getting chilly, so he rolled up the windows and flipped the dial to KLTZ. Number four on the charts was playing, "Running Bear." He drummed his fingers on his knees and sang along.

On the banks of the river stood Runnin' bear, young Indian brave
On the other side of the river stood his lovely Indian maid
Little white dove was her name, such a lovely sight to see
But their tribes fought with each other so their love could never be.

Was he Running Bear? And was Lois Little White Dove? What a dumb idea. He unwrapped a stick of Juicy Fruit, tossed the foil wrapper out the window. Stick to the *obvious!* He felt crazy-worried every time they'd met, only he didn't know how to stop.

He straightened the pleat in his white cords, smoothed the wrinkle from his pink V-neck sweater. He checked his glossy hair in the rear view mirror. He looked cool and confident—she did that for him.

Quietly, Lois slipped in the car. "Whew, I walked from the church." She waved her hand in front of her face. "I'm out of breath!"

He draped his arm over her shoulder, took in her white blouse, the top buttons undone. "What's your excuse tonight?"

"Just a church meeting." She slid over to his embrace. "I only have a few minutes." She tipped her head back to be kissed, smelled his clean skin, and touched her tongue to his lips.

He nuzzled her and spoke softly near her ear. "There's a rumor around school about us." She gave him a pouty look. "No one knows except Mag. And she doesn't know everything."

"Lois, this is crazy! I can't get caught *now*—our team is just coming together. I can't let 'em down." He retreated to his side of the bench seat. "We're working together like a machine. Pass, pass, shoot! Dribble, dribble, shoot. Coach said we're going to be a real threat to the big guys, and he said I could wear my feather headdress for the warm up. Can you picture that? Can you hear the war whoops and the drums?"

"Basketball's the last thing *I* want to talk about. Let's not waste our time!" Lois turned up the radio. "Dream Lover" filled the night air. "Dance with me." She pulled him from the car. "I love this song!"

They swayed into each other, and did a long, slow dance on the uneven ground. When she stumbled, he held her closer until their bodies merged into limbs, lips and music. When they broke apart, he ran down the levee and feigned a jump shot into a spreading birch tree. His polished loafers shed a dull gleam in the moonlight.

One long kiss later, Lois said, "Take me to my car. It's on Second Street by the church."

He grabbed her hand. "Let's not meet for a while. It's too risky!"

She slid out of the car without a word, just a look over her shoulder and a blown kiss that promised more.

Later, he cruised Front Street mouthing the familiar tune.

Runnin' bear dove in the water, little white dove did the same

And they swam out to each other through the swirling stream they came

As their hands touched and their lips met, the ragin' river pulled them down

Now they'll always be together in that happy hunting ground.

Chapter Twenty-Two

After Bobbi left, a loud knock sounded on the salon door.

"Hi, Patsy." Lois stepped inside. "I need a quick do. Big plans. Can you fit me in?"

Patsy nodded. "I should be closed. Although for you, I'll make time for a quick wash and set."

"That's perfect." Lois settled herself in the shampoo chair and exhaled slowly. "Soap it up twice with *really* hot water."

"Will do." Patsy scrubbed her scalp and gave her a neck massage.

"Oh, God, that's heavenly. I needed this!"

"Going out tonight?"

"Maybe," Lois said. "Tomorrow night for sure."

Patsy pondered. This was a perfect time to bring up her uneasiness about Bobbi. How to start?

While she was sectioning Lois's hair, rolling in the curlers, she began. "Bobbi picks up things fast—she's a real helper in the shop."

Lois opened the current issue of *Silver Screen.* "Is that right?"

"I like having her around. She's funny and cute."

Lois licked her finger and turned the page. "She's a brat at home!"

Patsy put her under the dryer with her magazine, thinking that Lois was damn lucky to have a daughter.

Patsy lifted the dryer hood.

Lois fanned her red face with her hand. "Hotter than Hades under there."

"Sorry," Patsy said. "I had it on high because you're in a hurry. I know the team doesn't play tonight. Coach will have the night off, and you can have a leisurely dinner."

"Are you kidding?" Lois examined her nails. "He never takes a night off! He'll go to Opheim or Williston to ref. And tomorrow night he has an Elks Club initiation. Just the guys."

"It's a man's world," Patsy said.

"Not for you, owning your own shop and all. Must be nice to set your hours—to do what you please in your free time."

"Who has spare time?" Patsy put her hands on her hips. "I have to make this place pay."

Lois swiveled the styling chair. "My first thought in the morning is what to fix for supper. And what to pack in the lunches for the girls and Coach every day. Tuna, egg salad, bologna? If I laid all the meals I've fixed end-to-end, they'd reach China! Honestly, if I never even drove by, let alone entered another grocery store, I'd die happy."

"I didn't mind making meals when I was married." Patsy said, "Maybe, it was easier as I had no kids. And I worked, although my hubby didn't like it. Unfortunately, it may have split us up."

"That's right, you're divorced."

"Twice, actually. I think I'm still in love with Ord, my second husband." It felt good to say it out loud and own it. No point in even thinking about other men, especially married ones like Coach.

Patsy folded her styling cape. "Would you rather be single?"

"I don't know." Lois picked up the emery board from the desk and filed a snag. "I've never worked or been on my own. I had the chance to go to college. Instead, I got married the summer after high school."

"The girls will be gone soon, and then you can have a break."

"Not soon enough! Marlene's a good kid, not like Bobbi!"

"Bobbi turned me down on working tomorrow, just when I needed the help. Actually, I'm quite worried about her—she seemed upset."

"I haven't noticed anything."

"I know it's not my business. Just thought I'd mention it."

Lois closed her magazine. "What did she tell you? Anything about me?"

Patsy couldn't divulge that Bobbi was upset about her parents' fights, and that she was especially scornful of her mom's behavior.

"Typical teen complaints. I got a strong feeling more was going on. She mentioned her friends," Patsy said. "Are they fighting?"

"Your guess is as good as mine."

"Also something about driving her boyfriend in a convertible."

"She's not allowed to drive that teacher's car! I don't know why she wants to drive. I don't, and I'm perfectly happy."

Patsy let that go. Who wouldn't want to be behind the wheel of a fancy Chevy convertible?

Lois tucked a curl behind one ear. "Do you like these earrings? What was that about Bobbi's boyfriend?"

Patsy considered her answer. She'd already said too much. "A guy on the basketball team. Actually, it sounded more like a crush."

"Nobody on the team would be interested in a kid like her. That's way out of her league!"

"I got the feeling she's about to do something rash."

As Lois made out her check, she said, "Bobbi's my problem, not yours." She handed the check to Patsy. "Tonight my daughter's going to a church retreat—I'm going to have a peaceful weekend for a change."

Chapter Twenty-Three

1955

Talking to Bobbi, as well as cautioning her against doing anything rash, reminded Patsy of what she'd done. It was her own selfish act that had sunk her marriage to Ord. Patsy remembered every shameful detail.

It had happened on a Thursday morning. The bacon smell and the runny eggs made her gag. The radio was announcing the weekly grocery specials. What could she make for supper that she already had in the house? In her plan, there was no time for grocery shopping. She was ready to go before Ord finished breakfast.

"What's your rush?" He put down the newspaper. "How are you doing this morning? I didn't hear you vomiting."

"I'm not sick for a change, just got cramps." She rubbed the small of her back. "Maybe, not real cramps, just a backache."

"Why don't you stay home?"

"I'm going to Havre to take my licensing test. I've got to have it to continue working at Ruth's. I may be a little late coming home."

"Well, don't do too much." He patted her on the behind. "I'll stop off at the bowling alley. I can get in a couple of games. Where are my shoes?"

"Try the back porch. I think I put them in your bowling ball bag."

"Bye." Patsy hesitated in the doorway. "Guess I'll get going then."

She returned to the table and dropped a kiss on his head. What if she died and never saw him again? The urge to cry was strong, and she had to hurry out.

The car ride seemed to take forever. She pushed the speed up to eighty as the telephone poles flashed by. The prairie was brown and lifeless this time of year. She saw two tiny antelope. They lifted their heads as the car sped by and seemed to plead for food. In late winter they came to backyards for garbage to get them through until spring. It was sad when the neighborhood dogs took them down.

Eventually, she saw the Canada sign with the arrow-pointing north. The turn off to the Indian reservation was in two miles. There she saw a cluster of white crosses. One, two, three, four, five. She shuddered. Five people had died there.

A couple of miles later the road turned to gravel, and the car slithered from side to side. She reduced her speed and checked her watch. How long would it take? When could things return to normal?

Growing up, all she wanted was getting a job so she could take care of herself, and that plan did not include having children. When Ord had said she could only work until she was in a family way, she was afraid to tell him how she felt. Would he have left her?

She certainly didn't want to be pregnant right now, as she was almost through with her training. Her experience losing the baby had made her terrified of another pregnancy. Also, the years caring for her sisters had put her off motherhood. She loved working at the salon, and imagined opening her own shop.

Around the last curve the box of super size Kotex slid to the floor as she reached the house at the end of the road. It had wood siding that badly needed paint, and shades drawn on all the windows. There was a washing machine on the porch along with parts of a car engine. She knocked. The front room seemed empty, and she could hear a radio from the back. The woman who answered the door looked far too young.

"Come into the kitchen. I'm setting things up."

"Are you Wanda?"

"Yes. I don't need to know your name. You can pay me now."

Patsy fished in her purse and counted out sixty-five dollars. Her tips for an entire year. "How many times have you done this?"

Wanda shoved the money into her back pocket. "More than I can count. How far gone are you?"

"Two months. I had one pregnancy eleven years ago that ended with a stillborn baby."

Wanda dropped some things into a boiling pot on the stove. She covered the kitchen table with an old sheet.

"Are you sure about the two months?" She struck a match for her cigarette. "I don't want any surprises."

"I know exactly when it happened."

"Okay. Take off your things, hop up here, and I'll see for myself."

Patsy removed her jacket, skirt and blouse. She hesitated at her underpants.

"Everything off. Don't worry, we're alone." She handed Patsy an old bedspread. "Wrap this around you."

She lay back on the table. Her legs dangled off the edge, and Wanda told her to scoot back a little.

"I'm going to check you first, then we'll get started."

Patsy felt cold hands spreading her legs and entering her body. She flinched.

"You've got to hold still," Wanda said, and her face appeared between her knees. "*Very* still."

"I'll try." She pulled the bedspread around her. The room was freezing like it was when she'd delivered her dead baby.

Wanda pushed something inside her. The pain staggered her, and Patsy flinched again. "Sorry. I can't help it." The tears rolled out of her eyes.

Wanda shook her head. "You white women. Can't take it, can you? I'll get you a drink."

"Thanks." Patsy's voice quavered. She gulped the liquor. It was not just a drink, more like a cupful. It seared her throat.

Wanda lit a cigarette and left it burning in the ashtray. From under the sink she pulled out a garbage pail and set it by the table. She began again.

Patsy willed her body to be motionless. She cast her eyes around the room. Concentrated on the details to take her mind off the pain. The walls were a dirty tan with long, jagged strips of peeling paint. A cord with a naked bulb dangled over the table. She kept her body quiet and still felt dizzy. The alcohol was working—she didn't care about the pain. She examined a crack in the ceiling that started in one corner winding around like a line on a map to her own time and place.

Abruptly, the hooch rose up in her throat.

Wanda handed her a small bowl. "Don't get up. Puke in here."

With each wave of nausea, Patsy heaved into the bowl. She heard groaning, her own voice from far away and a crunching sound as she passed out.

"It's over. You can go." The words seemed like they were coming through a long tunnel.

"I can't get up." Her limbs felt weighted down by heavy quilts.

"You're on your own, then. I've got to go to town."

Patsy heard car keys jingle. Then a door slammed.

She needed to get out of here. Slowly, she sat up. The pail was gone, and she had a pad between her legs. She touched one foot to the floor, then the other, and inched her way over to her clothes. Still nauseated, she kept gagging and burping the whisky. Her pelvic area burned.

Her car keys were where she'd left them, in the ignition. She sat, waiting for her head to clear. In the rear view mirror her face looked bloodless, the pallor of her skin frightening. Did something go wrong? She could hardly lift her hands to the steering wheel.

She drove in a daze, managing to reach the main highway. With the heater on high, she finally got warm. It was only two o'clock, a bit early to get home from the test. However, Ord wouldn't know what time she arrived as he'd still be at work.

She crept into the house and into bed, under the covers with her clothes on and was sound asleep when Ord got home.

He stood in the bedroom door. "Saw your car out front. Taking a nap?"

"I'm just tired."

"What happened? You look terrible."

"I've had a problem."

He sat on the bed.

"The cramps started last night, like I said." She began the story she'd prepared. "Not bad, just a dull ache. Then, during the drive I felt heaviness, and still, I made it to the beauty school in Havre. The test went okay. I was concentrating so hard, I forgot about the cramps.

"On the way out of town, the pain was something awful. I pulled into a filling station, and locked myself in the women's restroom. Blood poured out, and I flushed the toilet again and again. When I got home, I went right to the doctor's office. It's bad news, I'm afraid." She took his hand. "I've lost the baby."

He stared at her from the doorway. "I knew something was

going on. You sure weren't thrilled about having a baby. Tell me the truth—did you get an abortion?"

She'd never been a good liar. "I did what I thought was best."

His eyes were cold, and he didn't touch her. They didn't talk the next few days, although he brought her meals and helped her to the bathroom. He also called Ruth and said she needed a few days off.

Patsy could feel the door closing on their life together. She thought of explaining again. Mostly she just went over things in her mind. Could she have kept that first baby alive? She imagined braiding her little girl's hair, and teaching her to sort the curlers in the shop.

She knew better than to plead her case to Ord. She tried anyway, when he brought her lunch, macaroni and cheese on a tray.

"This is good." Patsy took large bites. "Thanks."

"I just followed the instructions on the box."

"Ord? Sit for a minute. Talk to me, please. I'm so sorry—it wasn't the right time. I had a real bad experience with my first pregnancy."

He put his face in his hands and cried. His grief broke her heart. She reached for his hand, and he brushed it away. Then, she began to cry.

He blew his nose. "You know how much I wanted kids."

"I got scared that the same thing would happen again. That the baby would die inside me. Just give up and die."

"You're my wife, and you lied to me. You killed our child." He choked back another sob. "Why didn't you talk to me about how you were feeling? We could have figured something out. I'd have gotten you help with your problem. We could have seen a specialist."

"I'm sorry. I panicked." She put her hand on his arm, "I just need some time. We could try again after I get my hours for my license. Can you forgive me?"

Later that week, when she was up and around, he met her in the kitchen.

"I'm sorry, I've thought about it, and I can't excuse what you did. I'm sorry, I'm trying, but I can't forget it. Here's some money to set you up in your new place." He handed her an envelope. "It's not much, and you can ask me for more when you need it."

"Please don't leave me." She put her arms around him. "We love each other, we can work things out."

After he left, the kitchen felt so empty. Even the radio was grim. More snow and freezing rain. She never imagined that Ord would be so devastated. She'd only been thinking of herself. That was no way to act in a marriage.

Her tears and grief overwhelmed her. She put her head down, and she wept. Later, when she felt calmer, she called Ruth.

"Ruth," she choked back a sob, "Ord's left me. Can you pick me up?"

>>>><<<<

Patsy had been on her own for two months. The last customer had gone. The radio played "Oh Lonesome Me," and Ruth hummed along. The sun had just set, but neither woman had bothered to turn on the lights.

"They upped my rent five dollars a month." She snapped the styling capes as she folded them.

Ruth rubbed lotion into her hands, "I wish I could help, but the shop's not bringing in enough for us both to work full time."

"Maybe we can be open a couple of nights a week. I wouldn't mind working in the evenings. Better than going home to an empty place."

Ruth put her arm around Patsy's shoulders. "Maybe he'll change his mind. I know how Ord felt about you."

"Don't hold your breath." Patsy shrugged free. "Here's another idea. I'm thinking of adding a home service. You know, for shut-ins and old people, or we could expand our operation here. There's lots of empty space on Main Street."

"Good God, you *have* been thinking."

"I can't sleep—my mind didn't shut off at all last night. I already called on an old folks home this morning. I have an appointment today at five-thirty. I'll charge a little more to make up for the gas and lugging my equipment."

"What about the hair dryer?"

"I've already ordered a portable."

"Good for you. For now you can drive my car. I'll get Ray to drop me off."

Patsy waited in the outer office. Once in, she made her pitch to Mr. Olson, the owner of Valley View Nursing Home.

"I'm starting a mobile beauty shop. You must have ladies that need haircuts and perms. I can do haircuts for men, too. I'm sure that most of your residents don't get out much"

"We don't have the space for a beauty shop."

"I can go to their rooms. That way, it will be more private."

He looked over his glasses at her. "Is that right? I'll give you a call next week."

A couple of weeks later she had only three appointments in the evenings and a couple of shampoo and sets at the rest home. She'd taken one hundred and fifty of the two hundred dollars from Ord and bought a used Plymouth. It was in good shape, and came with a set of tire chains for winter. The rest of the money went for utilities, rent and curtains for the trailer. Today, almost broke, she was on her way for a few groceries.

She noticed Ord's truck as she parked. She grabbed a basket and wheeled it up and down the aisles. Where was he? Her heart was racing. Over the shelves she spotted his favorite baseball cap by the bakery. She fluffed her hair and threw back her shoulders. He was there, but not alone. A woman with dishwater blonde hair, wearing a gray skirt and worn-down sandals, stood beside him.

"Get those cinnamon buns," Patsy heard her say, "for Sunday's breakfast."

She sat in her car, her hands trembling. Sunday breakfast. Bacon, fried eggs and toast. That's what Ord liked *her* to fix.

Suddenly, she craved ordinary things. Sitting at the kitchen table with Ord, peeling potatoes and listening to the news, the grain prices, the grocery ads, and the sales at J C Penny. Then on Thursday, the thump of paper hitting the porch. She would read every word—sometimes out loud to Ord. He'd stir his coffee and remark on any unusual item.

God, she missed him.

Ruth spotted her tears. "What's going on?"

"I saw Ord buying groceries with a woman."

"Sorry, I should have warned you. Do you want to know something about her? Would that help? She's not as pretty as you, that's for sure." Ruth resumed her work.

"I didn't think he'd find a girlfriend so fast."

Ruth flipped open the account book. "I've heard things from Mildred and Ethel, you know how they gossip. Ord met her at the dime store. Apparently, she's a widow with a six-year old girl. You know how Ord *likes* kids."

"Those old biddies! I wish all their hair would come out with the curlers! Just fall on the floor like snow!"

Ruth chuckled. "Then we *would* lose their business. And, heaven knows, we need plenty right now."

Patsy crossed her arms over her chest. "How are the books? Is my extra work paying off?"

Ruth handed her a check, "Sorry, still down, despite your efforts. Have you considered asking Ord for something to tide you over?"

Patsy gave her a withering look. "I'd rather die!"

"What about your nursing home business?"

"Starting, but slow."

Patsy hurried to the car. Totally depressed, she did something crazy and headed for Sam's Supper Club.

She sat in a back booth, feeling conspicuous. She'd never been in there without an escort. After hearing a woman at the bar order a Tom Collins, she'd gotten one for herself.

"Steak," she announced to the waitress. "Salad with French dressing, a baked potato with sour cream and a side of onion rings."

Her head hurt like she was getting a migraine. Why was she doing this? She only had twenty bucks; no gas in her car and rent was due.

She ate every scrap. Lately, most of her meals had been thrown together on the trailer's one burner stove. This was real food.

"Hi," the woman at the bar who'd ordered the Tom Collins gave her a little finger wave.

"Hello," Patsy waved back. The woman came over. She was dressed in a tight black skirt, ruffled white blouse and was quite pretty with ocean blue eyes, except for the furrow between her brows.

"I'm Sheri," she held out her hand.

"Patsy. Are you from around here?"

"You could say that. I've been around for a while."

They small talked about the unusually warm weather, the new

Doris Day movie, and the size of the mosquitoes in McCone County.

"Your hair is nice," Sheri touched her own split ends. "Where do you get it cut?"

"At Ruth's. The beauty shop across from the courthouse. In fact, I work there."

"You're a beautician? No wonder you look so good." She hid her hands in her lap. "Your nails look great, too."

"I'd love to do *your* hair. I could tone down the color and make it more natural." Patsy wrote on a napkin. "Here's my phone number."

"I've been doing the color myself." She looked embarrassed.

"I can tell. You do a pretty good job, but I have chemicals not available to the public. Why don't you come in this week? I'll make time for you."

"I really can't leave the ranch."

"Why?"

"I'm busy, so busy. Plus," she whispered, "he don't like us to come to town."

"You're here tonight."

"I had to meet someone who didn't show."

Patsy was mystified. "Well, I could come to you tomorrow or the next day. I'm just starting to do services away from the shop."

"That's good." Sheri stood. "I'll call you with directions."

The next day Patsy sat at her desk until six. The last customer had left, and she didn't feel ready to go home yet. She tallied up her receipts for the week. Better, but not enough. What was she going to do? How was she going to be on her own and support herself? Then Sheri called.

"I can see you tomorrow. Take the Fort Peck Highway. Right after the Milk River Bridge, turn left. There's no sign, but the mailbox says Palomino Ranch. Go about four miles. The road's not paved, but it's pretty smooth 'cause it's well traveled. Park around back, and I'll be watching for you. About ten tomorrow morning?"

"Sounds good. I'll bring my equipment."

Patsy was intrigued. Maybe Sheri had a hard-nosed husband. Maybe he didn't want a looker like her out of his sight.

It felt good to be driving, and for once she didn't think of money. She sang to herself on the drive. It would be fun to have a friend for a movie or just to meet for coffee.

The car rattled over the cattle guard, then crossed a creek. Patsy rolled down her window. The hickory leaves shimmered in the light breeze. The ranch house was two stories and freshly painted. On the front porch sat an old sofa and a couple of wooden chairs. Around back was a pick-up.

Sheri invited her into the kitchen. She wore a flowered kimono and had deep bags under her eyes.

"I didn't get much sleep." Sheri yawned. "We had a group of rough-necks from Miles City. Thought they'd never leave." She pulled the wrapper around her and sat at the table. "Can I get you a cup of coffee?"

"Okay." Patsy settled her stuff on the floor. They must have had some kind of a party, she thought.

Sheri lit up and dragged deep. Her robe gaped open, and Patsy caught a glimpse of a creamy breast. Another young woman wandered in. She looked young, like late teens. Her hair was messy, her lipstick spread around her mouth like a smear of jam.

"What a night," she said, "I got the same cowboy twice. Thought he'd never finish." She giggled. "But he gave me a nice tip. Is this the beauty operator?"

It finally clicked. *The Palomino*. Patsy had heard it whispered about at the shop. And she remembered how one of Ronnie's friends had dared him to go. She had been pretty stupid not to get it. However, she hid her surprise, and made herself act normal, not like she was standing in the kitchen of a whorehouse. With real prostitutes. With women who traded sex for money.

"I'm Jenny." The younger one held out her hand.

Patsy shook her hand. "Hi, I'm Patsy. I brought my equipment. Haircut anyone?"

"Yes." Sheri looked at her nails. "And a manicure."

"The same for me plus a pedicure." Jenny helped Patsy unpack the hair dryer and set it up on the kitchen table.

Patsy brushed Sheri's hair, set a chair in front of the kitchen sink, and tipped it back. Sheri sat down with a sigh.

"I love to have someone wash my hair. It's been so long."

Patsy soaped her twice and dug in with her nails all the while thinking about where she was. Both women seemed so normal like they lived down the street, and would come over for a cup or two. Well, maybe not Jenny. She'd still be in high school.

"How long have you been here?" Patsy asked Jenny.

"More than a year. Dropped out of school, and then my step-father chased me away. Or I should say, he chased me around the house, and I moved in with a friend. I started to wait tables, but this job pays a hell of a lot more."

"Is that right?" Patsy pushed cotton between Jenny's toes.

"Enchanted Pink. Put it on thick." Jenny giggled. "I made four thousand dollars last year."

Patsy felt sad. Prostitution paid better than the best jobs for women like teaching or secretarial work.

Three weeks later, Patsy had made two trips to the ranch. She'd been averaging twenty dollars a visit, and felt good about making her rent.

Sheri opened the door in a trim shirtwaist dress and pumps. "Boss is here today." She seemed subdued, and sat quietly at the table until Jenny came in.

Brushing Jenny's thick curls, Patsy didn't notice the man in the doorway until he coughed.

His presence filled the room. Dressed in black pants and a black shirt with pearl snaps, a black bolo tie, a Stetson hat, tooled leather boots and a silver buckle the size of a pie plate, he was pretty much the cowboy in charge.

"So, you're the gal doing the fixin?" he asked.

She held out her hand. "Yes."

He ignored her hand and draped his arm over her shoulders. "I'm Axel. Want to try out for a job at the ranch?"

Patsy took a step back, inadvertently inhaling his rancid breath. "I'm a licensed beautician."

"You could make more working for me." He looked so sinister with his poppy-eyed stare, long sideburns and narrow lips, Patsy expected him to twirl his mustache. Except that he didn't have one. His sallow cheeks and upper lip were freshly shaved. He smelled of bay rum.

She shook off his arm and continued putting pin curls in Jenny's hair.

"Finish up," he said, rocking back and forth on his high heels. "These girls have customers. Time is money."

Patsy slowly ran a brush through Jenny's hair. "They need time off to look their best."

Axel fell quiet. He wasn't used to back talk. When he left the room, Patsy smothered her giggles in Jenny's hair. "Is he always dressed like that? And that belt buckle! Could it be any bigger?"

"Don't laugh at him." Jenny looked serious. "He'll take it out on us."

"I can't—" Patsy collapsed with giggles, "can't help it."

Jenny put her hand over her mouth.

Patsy gasped, "Without the ten gallon hat and boots, he's about my size. And I'm not very big!"

"Neither is he!" Sheri added. "Anywhere!" Which brought a fresh wave of laughter.

With her traveling service to Valley View Nursing Home, the Palomino and work at Ruth's, Patsy kept herself busy for the next couple of years. Her work at the care facility set her up with some nice elderly clients, and more importantly, they tipped generously. Mr. Olson, the owner, often helped her carry in her equipment, and he invited her to the dining room for coffee. She'd grown accustomed to their chats.

However, she was only making enough to pay her expenses. It was always on her mind how to make more. How long would her vision of opening her own place have to wait?

The first week of August, Patsy and Sheri were having a milk-shake in the back booth of the drugstore.

"I've got a problem," Sheri said, "Axel told me not to see you."

"Why would he do that?" Patsy rubbed her temple where she felt a headache starting.

"He said it would be better if I had girl friends at the ranch. We'd have more in common."

"He can't stop you."

"He can make it tough by sending me the worst guys. The ones that don't tip, and the ones who get rough."

"All the more reason to quit."

"I'll think about it." She pulled on her finger. "How are things with you?"

Patsy frowned. "I'm working like a slave. Wash, set, perm, cut, and comb out—I'm managing."

"Think you'll be able to have your own place? Or you could work with me."

"I don't think I can."

They sipped in silence. Sheri took out her compact and powdered her nose.

"What about that guy you're seeing?"

"Ed Olson? We're just friends, although I can talk to him."

"Do you miss your husband?"

Patsy picked at a hangnail. "Ord? More than you could imagine."

"Do you see him?"

"We spoke on the phone a couple of times. There were some details to be cleared up about his insurance. We didn't talk about my problem, and why we separated."

Sheri raised her eyebrows, "Your problem?"

"As much as I loved Ord, I just—I just couldn't have his child, couldn't take the chance, so I got an abortion without telling him and it broke us up. He wanted kids in the worst way."

"I don't get it. Don't you want a family someday?"

"Maybe, but I panicked because I'd had such a bad time with my first pregnancy when I was married to Ronnie. The baby's heartbeat stopped at eight months. The doctor didn't know why, and I *had* to carry it ten days before I finally delivered. During that time, I still looked like I was expecting. People would smile and ask when I was due. Some even patted my tummy." She put her hands on her stomach as if to protect what was no longer there. "It was agonizing! Was it my fault 'cause I didn't want to be pregnant?"

Sheri put her arm around Patsy. "I'm sure you did nothing to hurt the baby. Boy or girl?"

"A tiny girl." The pain of memory sliced through Patsy. Her infant's face had been wizened like an old man's, and the little thing had been as light as a pile of cotton balls.

"Well, I probably passed up a chance to have a red-haired baby,"

Sheri said. "The cowboy might've married me, but I didn't love him."

"Wanda. Did you go to her?" Patsy's face turned white. "She helped me."

"Twice. I got knocked up twice." Sheri turned to hide her tears.

Patsy crumpled her straw. "You have to quit."

A week later Patsy and Sheri sat in Patsy's kitchen. Sheri filed her nails, and Patsy read the *Gazette*. The window shades were down, the room cool and quiet. In the soft light, their hair in curlers, they could be schoolgirls.

"Did you tell Axel you were staying in town tonight?" Patsy asked.

Sheri yawned. "Are you kidding? I didn't say a word. He's gone to Miles City. It's Tuesday, so most of the guys are with their wives tonight. And the cowboys are still broke and hung over from the weekend. One of the girls can cover for me."

Sheri put down her nail file. "I think Axel's going to put the pressure on you to work at the ranch."

"How?"

"He has his ways, and they're not pleasant. Also, he can pull a lot of strings in the county—he has the goods on almost everybody."

"I don't think he can hurt me."

"Hope you're right."

Patsy rubbed her calves. "I did eight heads yesterday, three perms, two pin curl sets and three haircuts. Trying to make a living."

"I hate what I do, but I *did* rake in the bucks last year." Sheri licked her finger and smoothed an eyebrow.

"I don't think it's as hard as the beauty business."

"What do you know about it, anyway?" Sheri pushed on her cuticle with an orange stick.

"Well, I've been married two times. I guess I know a little."

"*Married*," Sheri said. "When you can say no, when you're with the same person all the time, and he's clean, and you'll see him at breakfast. And you don't have to pretend or smile."

"As much as I need the money, I don't think I could take it."

"You'd be surprised how many men are just lonely. One guy wanted me to clean my face with Pond's cold cream, so I smelled like his wife. Another wanted me to cut his toenails, because that's what his mother did."

"Isn't it boring? The same thing over and over every day." Patsy said.

"I've gotten beaten up twice." Sheri held out her right hand. "My little finger is still crooked." She rubbed hand cream on the spot.

Just then, a car door slammed. The women froze.

"Who's that?" Patsy mouthed.

Sheri whispered, "Oh, no!"

Axel burst into the room. "You lazy bitch! I never said you could have a night off." He pushed her toward the door. "I told you to stop seeing her. Unless she comes to the ranch."

Sheri jumped up. "Leave her out of it!"

He grabbed Patsy's arms and locked them behind her back.

"Quit it!" she yelled.

Axel twisted harder. For a short man he had plenty of muscle. Patsy groaned in pain.

"Don't hurt her!" Sheri screamed. "I'll go."

Axel pushed her out the door.

Patsy shivered like it was ten below zero in the trailer. She wanted to call Ord in the worst way. He'd know what to do. She picked up her phone. It felt cold in her hand, and she held it to her chest like it was a tiny baby. Then she gently replaced it in the cradle. *Can't*, she thought, *can't call him.*

Patsy and Ed were having coffee, after Patsy had done her ladies at the rest home.

"What's wrong?"

Patsy gripped her coffee mug. "Nothing."

"Bull. Something's bothering you."

"I shouldn't tell you, but it's my friend, Sheri." She lowered her voice. "She's in terrible trouble."

Ed made the motion of zipping his lips.

Tears came as Patsy started to talk. Ed put his hand over hers while she poured out the whole story.

It'd been a month since Patsy had heard from Sheri, and she was worried sick. When she called the ranch, Jenny had reported that Axel had locked Sheri in her room.

"I'll help," Ed said. "But we'll have to do this ourselves. The law's not going to mess with Axel. Do you know where her bedroom is in the house, and does it have a window?"

"Yes and yes."

"Let's go tonight. I'll pick you up at about ten."

"Okay, but Axel's dangerous. Do we need a gun?"

"I'm not starting a war—we're just doing a rescue."

They left Ed's car parked on the side of the gravel road, just past the Palomino mailbox. The late summer night was still warm, and the moon was low on the horizon. She reached for Ed's hand.

"Turn off the flashlight," she whispered. "They might see us. And be careful—the road's full of ruts."

"That's her window," Patsy pointed to the house. "There's a light on. Let's wait." They crouched under a lilac bush. Husks of dried but still fragrant blooms dusted their shoulders. Thin clouds obscured the moon. The light in Sheri's room dimmed.

"She must have a customer," Ed whispered.

A car started up and sped down the road. *Someone going home,*

Patsy felt sick at the thought, *probably to his wife and kids.*

Just then a coyote howled, and a dog barked.

"I forgot about the dog," Patsy whispered. "Here it comes."

A black lab barreled toward them.

"Hush, doggie," Ed coaxed him nearer.

The dog stayed about three feet away and barked. Someone came out on the front porch and whistled, and the dog ran back to the porch. Relief like warm bath water spread over Patsy.

"Good dog, Buster." It was Axel. "Good dogs don't chase coyotes." He let the dog inside, then slammed the screen door.

They waited and waited. It had rained the night before, and the smell of damp sage was as pungent as cat piss. The northern lights, like a sheer green curtain, wavered on the horizon. They didn't speak at all. Eventually, the mosquitoes found them. Patsy tucked her skirt around her legs, but she was soon scratching. About one-thirty in the morning, Sheri's light went out for good.

Ed stood, shaking the stiffness out of his legs. "Let's go."

They crept toward the house and crouched beneath Sheri's window. Patsy tapped lightly. Loud enough for Sheri to hear, not so loud someone else would notice.

Nothing happened, so Ed motioned for Patsy to try again. She hesitated when she pictured Axel's shotgun. He kept it on a rack over the back door—loaded. Patsy tapped again. She heard a groan and a rustle.

Sheri appeared in the window. Her hair was a rat's nest, and she looked scared.

"Patsy? Is that you?"

"Yes."

"I can't let you in. Axel checks my room."

"Crawl out the window *now*! Don't bother getting dressed. Ed's with me, and we'll get you out of here!"

Sheri hesitated. "He'll find me!"

"No," Ed said. "We'll get you somewhere safe."

The moon came out from behind the high clouds. Patsy gasped. Sheri's cheek was bruised, and she had a hell of a black eye.

"Are you waiting until he *kills* you?" Patsy spat the words.

Sheri disappeared. Patsy's eyes darted around the dark yard until Sheri came back in her robe, carrying her purse and shoes.

"Hurry," Ed said.

The three of them ran down the road, and piled in the car, totally out of breath. The women sat in the back and held hands as Ed drove. They took Patsy to her trailer where they grabbed some clothes for Sheri, and then listened to Ed's instructions.

"Sheri, I'm going to drive you to Havre. There's a bus in the morning that will take you home to Kentucky. I'll stay with you until it comes."

"Patsy, the first place he'll look is the shop. Make sure Ruth or someone is with you tomorrow. I'll call you when I get back."

Patsy was plain worn out as she started work in the morning. She'd stayed in her locked car until her first appointment arrived, per Ed's instructions.

Was Sheri safe? Axel was a devil. Maybe he'd come after Ed, or hurt Jenny to get revenge. She remembered the pistol she'd seen on his desk and the scars on his arms. He was a guy who had seen plenty of action. She felt helpless and weak. What would she do if he showed up? Ed wouldn't be back from Havre until noon at least.

She willed herself to concentrate on the heads in the shop. Just as she was mixing Bev's hair color, Axel barged in. The two ladies under the dryer dropped their magazines. He was dressed in his black clothes, and was vibrating with rage.

"Where's my whore?" He grabbed Patsy's shoulders and shook her hard.

Patsy winced. "Gone," she breathed. "You'll never see her again!"

Axel renewed his grip and twisted her to her knees.

"You're gonna pay for this, you meddling cunt!" He slapped her face and pushed her down between the styling chair and the sink. The ladies lifted their dryer hoods.

"Lordy, lordy, a *fight*!" Edna said.

Patsy grunted as she tried to get her feet under her, but Axel gave her a vicious kick.

She fell back with a groan, yelling, "Shit, shit, shit!"

On the table was a bowl of bleach. Patsy gripped its slippery edge and hurled it at Axel. The red plastic bowl hung in the air like a hot red sun, and then smacked him squarely in the chest. He jumped back as it splashed his face, arms, legs and even boots. While he frantically tried to brush off the sticky globs, Patsy crawled to the desk phone.

"Operator," she said. "Quick, send the sheriff to Ruth's Beauty Shop."

Axel grabbed the phone and tossed it across the room. He suddenly ran out of steam and screeched as the bleach burned his skin.

Just then Ruth arrived. She herded the frightened clients to the back room. "Wait here." She pushed Patsy into a styling chair and tossed a towel to Axel. "The sheriff's on his way."

Ruth stood between them, her arms out like a referee at a boxing match. Patsy sobbed. Axel cursed as he tried to wipe away the bleach.

When the sheriff arrived, Axel's natty cowboy outfit was covered with large white spots. His eye oozed and the bleach had stuck to one eyebrow and turned it blonde.

The sheriff and his deputy looked from one to the other with suppressed smiles. Patsy figured they knew Axel. They took him outside first to hear his story, and next they interviewed Patsy and talked to each other in low voices.

"No harm done," the sheriff told Patsy. "Axel won't charge you for new clothes, if you let this little disagreement end here. Apparently, you stole something valuable from him. Course, he can't prove it, but he knows his rights."

"*His* rights! That asshole bulled in here and slapped me around!" Patsy's voice was shrill.

"Okay, little lady, he didn't mean to lose his temper. Folks will vouch for him. Axel *is* pretty well-known around here."

Patsy was so mad she was dumbstruck. She stared at her boss, hoping she'd speak up, but Ruth remained quiet.

The sheriff hooked his thumbs in his belt. "Nice set up you've got here. I'm going to send my wife over for a haircut." He sauntered out.

"No charge for today, girls." Ruth ushered out the clients. They patted their newly set hair and twittered. They could hardly wait to tell the juicy story to their friends.

"God, what a mess." Ruth bustled around as Patsy held her head in her hands.

"Jesus, God, Ruth, he could have killed me. Look at my legs." She examined her shredded nylons.

"I doubt it. He has a temper, but he's not crazy. Everyone knows you helped Sheri get away. She had some powerful customers that will miss her, so there's nothing we can do." She massaged Patsy's bent shoulders. "Nothing if we want to stay in business."

Patsy glanced in the mirror. "I look like something the cat dragged in!" She'd never seen her face this way, pale as wedding dress white with leathery pouches beneath her eyes. "He was beating her."

Ruth shook her head. "You were lucky this time."

For the next two weeks the shop was slow. Patsy had an upset stomach every day as she forced herself to go through the motions and not acknowledge her doubts about the lack of business. She hoped that haircuts and color were put off during the summer due to swimming and vacations.

It was the end of the month before she got the bad news.

"I'm sorry, Patsy. You're my friend and such a good employee, but I'm going to have to let you go." Ruth brushed a ball of hair into the wastebasket.

"*What*? You're firing me?"

"Our clientele is way down. Word of mouth about the brawl here—I'm not making enough to pay you." She dusted the top of the desk. "Women are canceling appointments."

Patsy sagged in the styling chair. Her chest heaved, and she made no attempt to wipe her eyes or the snot that leaked from her nose. What was the use? "I can't stand it. I don't want to lose my job or our friendship." She waved her arms in the air, as if taking in the whole world. "Everything is gone—the baby, then Ronnie. And Ord—losing him nearly killed me!"

Ruth waited until the storm was over. Then, she took the broom and dustpan out of the closet.

"All water under the bridge, hon. You're a good hairdresser, so you can get a job someplace else. Axel's not going to forget this. You've got to do what he wants or leave town!"

Chapter Twenty-Four

Bobbi drove the bitchin' car, and nothing else mattered. She was through chanting all the worst swear words she knew—*shit, fuck, bitch, bastard and asshole.* Who cared that her mom was sneaking around with an Indian basketball player, that Donna and Rita hated her, or that her dad was dancing with a beauty operator? She was going overnight with Miss Bauer, whom she'd been forbidden to see, and she was driving her dream car! If her parents could break the rules, so could she.

The moon glowed white above the prairie. She swept by the black and yellow wheat fields. She kept the speed under eighty as homage to the white crosses for the highway dead, and kept the yellow line a perfect two feet from the car.

Miss Bauer—she kept forgetting to call her Jean—smoked, the fumes swirling out of her mouth. After an hour Jean relaxed into sleep with her narrow chin bouncing on her chest. Bobbi reached over and removed her sunglasses as they looked like they were going to be blown off. Sticking them on her own face, Bobbi vowed to get a pair of Ray-bans too.

Bobbi turned up the radio and sang along with "Love Me Tender." She ran her thumb and forefinger around the steering wheel, and petted the smooth leather seat, and admired her classy, rolling kingdom.

Jean guided Bobbi as she carefully backed the convertible into a space in the teacher's parking lot. They sauntered into the gym. She felt like a new girl, the mysterious girl, the one driving a convertible.

"Hi, Janice." She gave a big wave to a girl she'd met last year at a band festival. She didn't have to worry, no one here would report back to her parents.

Williston was behind at half time, twenty-five to thirty-eight. While the band played in the bleachers, they ate chilidogs and fries. Bobbi rolled each fry in ketchup and in mustard. Jean smoked a lot, dropping her butts into an empty Coke cup, and sipped from a flask. She poured whisky into Bobbi's cup.

The third quarter was a noisy blur. In the fourth, the Bulldogs got the ball and ran for a lay-up. When they made the winning basket, the band and the screaming caused Bobbi to cover her ears. Everyone in the bleachers jumped up and down, the thumps like car collisions. Jean hugged her like it was their personal victory.

"Let's drag Main," Jean said, "With the top down."

"That'd be so cool!" What a story she'd have to tell!

Only wait, Donna and Rita thought she was spending the weekend babysitting. And she told her mom and dad she was on a retreat with Pilgrim Fellowship, a special program for those interested in leadership positions, which she was not! Still, it was a smart plan anyway. Maybe she could tell Donna in secret about the car and the game, maybe in a year.

Bobbi steered the convertible behind the players' bus. Did the guys think she was someone important? They paraded up and down Main Street, making wide U-turns at the end of the block. She spotted Janice again at the corner and gave her a showy salute.

Jean slumped in her seat, letting her take the glory, she guessed.

Hours later, it seemed like, the bus turned back to the school and the parade was over.

"Want to go for coffee and pie?" Jean asked.

Bobbi was full. The French fries felt like a stack of wet straws in her stomach. Her eyes itched like when she, Rita, Donna had stayed up all night looking at the dirty pictures in her aunt's nursing books.

"Do you want pie?"

Bobbi suppressed a boozy belch. "I'm kind of full." It would be more exposure in the car, except she was sleepy.

"Let's head to the Star Motel where I reserved a room."

Bobbi parked and set the bags by the door while Jean checked-in. She yawned and scratched her head. Her hair felt like grandma's yarn basket. Did she remember to bring her hairbrush? She had packed in a great hurry, her mother's betrayal welling up in her throat like spoiled milk.

The room smelled of old blankets and Pine Sol. Two beds with worn chenille spreads divided the space. A small TV with rabbit ears, a bedside table with a lamp, and a desk filled the room. Bobbi straightened the lamp, fingered the burned hole in the shade.

Jean tossed her suitcase on the bed by the door. "Ever been in a motel before?"

"No, it's kinda dingy."

"Not so bad, a good price. If you liked the game, we can come again."

"What about the car? Should we put the top up?"

"We can do it in the morning. It's tricky, I need daylight." Jean took her toiletry kit from her suitcase. "I'll use the bathroom first."

Bobbi touched the squat black phone on the bedside table. She felt like calling someone. But who? She didn't want anyone to know where she was. What was happening at home? Were Mag and Mom planning to go to the meet tomorrow night at the Montana? Had anyone told her dad about Pretty Weasel? What a mess! Maybe she should've stayed home.

The lamp flickered, and she screwed the bulb a little tighter. Then she slumped on her bed.

Jean came from the bathroom in a plaid bathrobe and bare feet. She set her glasses on the desk by the car keys. "Aren't you going to brush your teeth?"

"I was feeling dizzy. I've never had whisky." She slowly sat up. "I feel a little better now. I'll wash my face."

In the bathroom, she buried her face in the flannel nightie that Grandma had made her for Christmas. It smelled like home.

She sipped water, peered into the mirror. She looked pale and tired. After squeezing a few zits, she washed her face again. Then she peed, quietly, letting a little out at a time. Could Jean hear? All she could hear was the TV. Was that *Perry Mason*? She hated that show.

She slipped under the bedspread as Jean turned off the TV and light.

Jean sat next to Bobbi on the bed. "You know, of all the girls, you're my favorite."

"I am? More than Rita and Donna?"

"You're a reader like I was at your age. I couldn't believe you actually read *Julius Caesar*. Even before it was assigned. Besides all that, you're kinda cute."

"I'm too skinny!"

Jean leaned in. "You've got nice little boobies."

Bobbi pulled the bedspread to her neck.

Jean put her hand on Bobbi's arm. "I want to help you with that tickle problem. What does your sis do?"

"When she touches my ribs, I'm helpless. I try to fight back, except I feel paralyzed. She keeps tickling me until I wet my pants or mom makes her stop."

"I think I can help you with that. It's mind over matter. Did I ever play bear with you?"

"What's bear?"

"I sniff you all over and if you move, I can maul you and take bites of you. You'll learn to stay very still when your sister tickles you."

"That's stupid, I'm not afraid of bears. I just don't want to wet my pants."

"Close your eyes."

Bobbi smelled Jean's dirty hair. It almost made her gag. In English class, all of the girls talked about the teacher's greasy hair.

Bobbi breathed through her mouth. Then she gave Jean a push. "I don't think this is going to work."

Jean touched her lightly on the chest. "Let me try it."

Bobbi felt too tired to protest. In fact, she'd never felt so exhausted. The lying to get out of the house, the raucous game, cruising main, the greasy food, and the booze—it was all too much.

Jean put her hand on the hem of her nightie. "I need bare skin. Isn't that what your sister does?"

"Sometimes, sometimes through my clothes."

"Are your eyes closed?"

"What does it matter? I can't see you, anyway."

Jean inched up Bobbi's nightie, and moved a hand to her ribs. "It helps you focus."

Could she just get the icky stuff over with? Like she'd do with the Novocain shot at the dentist? Bobbi stared out the back window. A tiny moon hung like a sliver from a baby's fingernail. She thought of the blue moon, a full moon, the moon made of green cheese, and the man in the moon.

Bobbi felt the hands, and still stayed with the moon. The fingers swept her ribs, circled her waist, stroked back and forth along the edge of her panties, then slipped under the elastic. Now her stomach became the moon, and the fingers explored the surface and the crater of her belly button. She felt powerless under the crawling fingers as they slid down her panties.

Bobbi jerked up. "I can't stand it! I'm too ticklish!"

Jean roughly pushed her down. "Yes, you can, it feels good, *good.*" Her voice was low and menacing like a dog's growl.

Again Bobbi smelled the hair, the whisky, and the stale smoke. She twisted away.

"Hold still," Jean commanded. "This will only work if you lie very, very still!"

Then she stretched out beside Bobbi. Through her open robe she ground her naked hips into Bobbi's side. "Do you feel it?" she asked loudly. "Do you *feel* it?" Her hot stinky breath puffed into Bobbi's face.

Jump, Bobbi thought, jump out of the car. Get away from the whisky breath and the grabbing. Like she'd done when one of the dads felt her up as he drove her home from babysitting. Only, she wasn't in a car any longer.

Jean inserted her bare leg between Bobbi's. Pinned by the strong legs, Bobbi felt panic rise in her throat like vomit. Jean's hand shot to Bobbi's naked crotch. Sharp fingers probed inside her. The pain made Bobbi gasp as the ragged fingernails tore her tender skin.

Jean mumbled dirty words: *fuck, dick, pussy, cunt!* Her hips rolled, pitched, and she slammed her crotch into Bobbi's hip, threw her head back and spit out another stream of filthy words. Then, only then, did she pull her fingers out, relax her punishing grip on Bobbi's legs, and slide into the other bed.

Bobbi felt wet and sore. Tears rolled down her cheeks. What had happened? Was that blood down there? Afraid to move, she willed herself to be stock-still until Jean fell asleep, which she hoped wouldn't be long given the amount of alcohol she had drunk.

It was cold and dark, the moon gone from the window by the time puffing snores sounded from the next bed. Pulling her nightie down from her neck, she felt around for her panties. Then, she tiptoed to the bathroom, grabbed her toothbrush, her shoes, her clothes, and the car keys from the desk. It took forever to turn the doorknob, slide out, and shut the door. Only one-way out. She would steal the car.

Outside, everything was turning white. Several inches of snow had fallen. Bobbi raised her face to the sky, flakes landing on her eyelashes and lips. The car was dusted with soft white snow like a storybook scene. In contrast, Bobbi felt dirty and ashamed. After dusting the driver's seat and part of the windshield, she dressed hurriedly and drove to the highway before switching on the headlights.

Shifting from side to side on her sore bottom, she realized that tickling would *never* bother her again. There were far worse things. She felt like the time she'd stolen two bucks from her grandma's purse, like when she'd let the Olson baby cry while she gabbed on the phone, like when she'd sent the note around in science class, the note with the F word, signed with Diane's name. Only this was worse.

Halfway home at Poplar, Bobbi remembered that she was supposed to be gone all day. She parked behind the closed Dairy Queen. The car seemed safe, hidden from the highway. She fastened her jeans, tucked in her nightie, and pulled a sweater over it. Noticing blood on the car seat, turned pink by the snow, she quickly wiped it away and walked downtown.

In Highway Café, she ordered coffee and toast as she had only two dollars. She gripped the thick white cup until her hands thawed, and then she waited for the waitress to refill her cup.

Tugging on her hairnet, the waitress kept looking at Bobbi.

Honestly, did it show? Did the waitress know she'd lost her virginity by her walk or because of the way she moved her hips? What about those fast girls in high school, the ones that wore their boyfriend's class rings around their necks, bouncing up and down on their boobs? You could tell *they* weren't virgins. Was she like them now?

Bobbi tried to act nonchalant so the waitress wouldn't be suspicious. She pulled out the cigs and dropped the match in the ashtray. Then she scanned all the songs on the jukebox. She longed to hear "Wake Up Little Susie" or "True Love Ways."

This would be fun if Donna and Rita were here. Did they still hate her? What were they doing this weekend?

A few hours later, she reluctantly left her secluded booth for the bathroom. She was shocked to see more blood on her panties, and it hurt to pee.

She noticed a highway patrolman at the counter, drinking coffee. Crap, had Miss Bauer already reported the car missing? Were they looking for her? Jesus God, maybe she'd get arrested. She slipped past the patrolman.

It was snowing hard. However, she waited in the car until three o'clock. Again, she fumbled with cold fingers. How in the hell did the top work? She couldn't figure it out, but she eased onto the highway, anyway. Forty miles. Home in a couple of hours. It looked like she had just enough gas.

The heater, on high, only warmed her ankles. Her hands and ears were freezing. *Shit, Shit, Shitoosie,* how could had she have been so stupid? The drifts, carved by the wind, piled ever higher alongside the highway. Should she pull over and wait to die?

Cutting her speed to thirty, she didn't brake again after the back end fishtailed. Where were the road signs? Had she passed Wolf

Point? On and on she drove, the gas needle heading to empty.

Finally, she glimpsed a red and yellow light through the snow. The light disappeared, and then flickered again. A torch? Sometimes, when the fans heard on the radio that Bowman had won, they built a bonfire by the side of the highway to welcome the team bus. Then, they all caravanned to town. She wasn't the team, except it sure looked like a fire. Who would do that?

She rattled over a cattle guard, bump, bump, until she had no power, and the car coasted to a stop by the side of the road. She was out of gas.

Should she stay in the car or start walking? There was the Montana highway lost-in-the-snowstorm-rule, *Never Leave the Car!* Last winter, a family of five had stalled on the Opheim Highway. Following a fence, they thought they could make it to town. The next day they were found with their frozen mittens still clutching the barbed wire.

She climbed out into the blowing snow. No way was she staying with the car. Running toward the flickering, she yelled, "Who's there?"

"Bobbi, is that you? We're over here!!"

She stumbled toward the light on numb feet. Was the blaze for her? Two figures appeared in the dark, jumping and yelling. Rita and Donna screamed her name. They'd built the bonfire. *Jesus, Mary and Joseph*, she thought.

They were waiting for her!

Chapter Twenty-Five

"Where *were* you?" Donna and Rita begged.

The three girls sat crammed together in the front seat of Rita's car. The hugging, the laughing and the crying had stopped. The wipers flapped back and forth, clearing snow from the windshield. The heater poured out warm air.

Rita poked Bobbi with her elbow. "For shit's sake, tell us everything!"

"Hold on a sec." She finally asked, "How did you know I was coming?"

"You tell first!" Donna said.

"Okay." Bobbi vowed to herself, she'd only tell them the good stuff. The shameful thing she'd keep to herself.

"Miss Bauer invited me to Williston for a basketball game. She let me drive. I can tell you I was flying low in that classy chassis. It was *so* cool dragging Main, and I got to drink whisky."

Rita sucked on her wet mitten. "Yeah, we figured you were with her. She invited us, too."

"She did?" Bobbi was incredulous. "No way. She said I was her favorite!"

"After class, when she suggested we go to the game, I got called favorite, and later Rita did, too!"

"Is that true? Boy, am I dumb."

"Don't worry about it." Rita hugged Bobbi. "We were all dunces. She used that car as bait to take advantage of us."

"You got that right! Now your turn," Bobbi said. "How'd you know I went to the game? And when I was coming home?"

"Wait a second," Rita said, "Let's get back to town."

"What about Bauer's car?" Bobbi asked.

"*Leave it,*" Donna and Rita said in unison.

"Okay by me," she agreed. "I'm *never* going to drive it again!"

Rita carefully steered through the whirling snow and parked behind the closed grocery store.

"How'd you know I went to the game?" Bobbie asked again.

"To start with, Pasty was suspicious and called me. She definitely didn't buy the story about the church retreat," Rita said.

"Jeez, Patsy called?"

"Yeah," Rita said. "Then I heard my dad on the phone with your dad, saying something about Miss Bauer's stolen car. Like I said, we figured you'd gone with her. There's only one way home from Williston, and it was snowing hard, so we drove out, built the bonfire and waited for hours."

Bobbi sniffed back tears. "Thank you, God! Thank you, Patsy! You saved me! I love you guys!"

"So, where's Miss Bauer? Did you *steal* her car?" Rita pummeled Bobbi's arm. "Give now, give!"

Bobbi wiped her nose on her sleeve. "I left her in the motel. That creep. I hope I never see her again! I only went 'cause I found out something terrible about my mom, which I'll tell you later. I already told you about the game and dragging Main. Then, in the motel, Miss Bauer did something horrible, something I can't talk about."

Rita stared Bobbi down. "You can tell *us anything now* that we're friends again. Miss Bauer made us mad at each other. She split us apart with her car. And Bobbi, she just wanted to feel you up. Boy, oh, boy, I'm sorry that I even mentioned how ticklish you were, and how you hated it."

"That's exactly how it started last night, with a tickle lesson. Then she . . ." Bobbi bit her tongue, and couldn't go on.

Rita stroked her back. "Come on, tell us the rest."

Bobbi teared up, and then started bawling. She pushed her way out of the car and retched. Donna and Rita knelt beside her and held her hair back as the yellow slime spilled out. Her body shuddered as she emptied her stomach into the snow and choked out the last words.

"She felt me up like you wouldn't believe and did other icky things."

"It's not your fault!" Rita guided Bobbi to the car. "She fed you booze and trapped you!" Rita bit a fingernail. "My mom said they called her 'unnatural' at the school board meeting. Personally, I think she's queer."

"Really? Is she a homo, a real homo? Do we know any other queers?" Donna asked.

"There is that girl in our class who flies crop dusters and wears boy's jeans. Why, Bobbi," Rita persisted, "couldn't you have stayed in the motel and come home with her?"

"I was panicked and scared! And the worse thing, now . . ."

"What?" Rita and Donna chorused.

Bobbi hung her head and muttered, "I may not be a virgin. I feel wet and sticky, and have lots of blood on my panties."

"Does your stomach hurt?" Rita asked.

"Like crazy." Bobbi rubbed her abdomen.

"You silly. That's not from the things she did to you." Donna clapped her on the back. "It's your period! Finally!"

Just then they heard sirens and the Sheriff's car zoomed by on the highway.

"Good God almighty!" Bobbi said. "I almost forgot about the meeting. What time is it?"

Donna rubbed the foggy dashboard clock. "Around ten, I think. What meeting?"

"Quick, we have to go to the Montana Bar. My mom is meeting Pretty Weasel, and there might be trouble."

"We heard he had a thing with an older woman, we thought it might be Mag Henderson," Rita said. "Jeez, your *mom*? I thought *you* had a crush on Pretty Weasel."

"I thought about him every day. I wanted to give him a ride in her convertible. God, he was a dreamboat!" Bobbi said.

"Wasn't your mom there the day you met Pretty Weasel?"

"Right," Bobbi said, "she wore her fancy sundress and red lipstick."

"Are you sure it's her and not Mrs. Henderson?" Donna asked. "It'd be crazy for a player to hook up with the Coach's wife."

"One night I followed them," Bobbi admitted. "They slipped in the back door of the Montana Bar. Another time, I think I saw my mom in his car."

"Your mom stealing your boyfriend? That's seriously *sick*!" Rita gunned the motor.

Chapter Twenty-Six

Mary Agnes arrived in the Montana early Saturday night, anticipating the meet. Seated by the back door, she was prepared to race out at ten.

Spring snow had driven everyone inside; they were packed body to body. The jukebox glowed neon red and green in the corner and Hank Williams mourned, although it was hard to hear, the chatter was too loud.

Pretty Weasel's name kept coming up. The Indians hadn't had a player on the varsity for years. After the squad had beaten Great Falls, everyone was excited about the team's chances. It had been fourteen years since they'd gone to State, and the mood was upbeat. Thirsty drinkers were lined up double at the bar, and most of Saturday night was still to come.

Mary Agnes worried about the proposed meet-up between her son and Lois. It had better be the last time! How stupid, an Indian teen and a married white woman together. It had to end. She'd gotten herself into fixes—sent away to a federal Indian school, pregnant at fourteen, except those problems were thrust on her. Pretty Weasel and Coach's wife were making their own mess.

Wanda and Dede sat in a back booth with a couple of guys.

"Sit with us, Mary Agnes," Wanda yelled. "We're buying."

"No!" she yelled back. Tonight, she didn't intend to drink. She didn't want Pretty Weasel to feel ashamed of his mom.

Ben and Martha, whom she'd lived with when Pretty Weasel was a baby, came to her side.

"Your kid's doing great," Martha said.

"He's the star center." Mary Agnes smiled. She hoped they weren't going to take some credit for his success. After all, years ago they'd kicked them both out of their house trailer.

Ben lifted his beer can and clinked glasses. "Congrats on his success! Remember when he cried all the damn time! Made us crazy."

"I tried to keep him quiet," Mary Agnes said. "He didn't get enough to eat."

"Goddamn, it seems like just yesterday he was a baby, and now he's playing ball!" Wanda shook her head in disbelief.

It didn't seem like yesterday to Mary Agnes. It seemed like centuries ago that she'd been pregnant and had to leave the Indian school. She had to dig deep to recall the details of Pretty Weasel's birth and her brief time with him.

Chapter Twenty-Seven

1942

Mary Agnes left Indian school in early spring. She'd refused to wait inside the station that day, although an hour passed before the eastbound train arrived.

She pulled her hand-me-down coat tightly around her, and turned her back to the wind. It rocked her, and she welcomed its force. She wished it would blow her across the tracks, over the grain elevator, clear to the next valley, the next and the next.

On the train she'd grabbed a vacant seat and huddled against the wall. The vibrations of the train rocked her into a kind of stupor. She dozed until a familiar sensation overcame her. Frantically locking the restroom door behind her, she bent over the toilet and retched.

Back in her seat, she started thinking about Leo. When would he notice her absence? Almost every day she'd met him in the boiler room, as it was still too cold outside. They would snuggle into an old green army blanket and plan their next break out.

Earlier that day, Mrs. Francis surprised her by calling her out of recess and taking her to the dorm.

"Pack your things, Mary Agnes. You're going home. We're through with you here."

"I have a history test this afternoon."

"Now, Mary Agnes." She handed her student a large paper sack. "We're putting you on the afternoon train."

"Why?"

"You know why, Mary Agnes. Of course, you know."

"It's not my fault." Mary Agnes clenched her fists. "I couldn't help it."

"I don't want to hear any excuses. Hurry up so you won't miss the train."

Mary Agnes stuffed her notebooks, toothbrush, and a few articles of clothing into the sack.

"Here's your train ticket and lunch. I've given you two peanut butter cookies. I know they are your favorite."

She couldn't stop the tears. "Can I talk to Leo before I go?"

Mrs. Francis put her hand on Mary Agnes's shoulder. "Afraid not. You've spent too much time with him already—altogether too much time."

"How will he find me in Montana?"

"You can write to him here at the school."

The school. Finally, she was leaving after almost two years. She gazed at the flat prairie and the wheat fields speeding by. The remaining snow looked patchy. In some areas the winter wheat poked green through the black dirt. She found herself looking for the antelope she had seen on the way to the school. How silly, she thought, some hunter has probably bagged him, cut him into chops, steaks, and ground the rest into sausage.

How many times had she wished to ride this train to home? She'd longed for this moment every day. Some days, she'd thought she would die if she couldn't see Auntie and play basketball with Gail. She wanted to be home, only not like this—not three months gone, and not without Leo.

After the long journey, she stood on the platform, feeling grubby and tired. Nobody was there to meet her. The bars, the muddy trucks with snow chains on the tires, everything looked the same. The street was slushy with spring snow and water ran in the gutters. She felt the unseasonably warm Chinook wind.

She pulled her coat around her to hide her stomach, and headed to her Auntie's. It was only six blocks.

Auntie answered her knock and gave her a hug as Mary Agnes broke down in tears.

"Now, now, it can't be so bad."

"Oh, Auntie, it was really terrible. They didn't want us to be Indians anymore. We couldn't speak Crow; we had fleas in our beds, and look at my legs. Here are the scars from being whipped."

"I didn't know it was so bad. You never wrote to me."

"Yes, I did!" Mary Agnes sobbed. "I wrote and told you everything. I bet they didn't mail my letters."

"You must be tired. Why don't you take a bath and I'll make supper? Then we can talk."

"Oh, my gosh, a bath! All the girls had to share one slimy shower."

Mary Agnes stood in her old room. Pictures of friends framed the mirror. Gail and Wanda grinned for the camera. What would they think of her now?

She opened the closet. There were her basketball shoes and the medicine bundle she wore inside her socks at the games. She clutched the shoes to her chest and slumped to the floor. There'd be no more basketball for her.

They talked at supper. The agency had notified Auntie to expect Mary Agnes and why.

"So you're pregnant," Auntie said, "like mother, like daughter. Who's the father?"

Mary Agnes helped herself to another piece of fry bread. "What does it matter? It's my fault. Please don't tell anyone how stupid I've been."

"You can only hide it for awhile. I should have kept you here. It's the BIA that's stupid, not you!"

Mary Agnes put her head in her hands and tears flowed between her fingers.

Auntie patted her. "You'll be okay, we can figure something out. Have another piece of fry bread. I made it just for you."

Mary Agnes pushed away her plate and burped. "Excuse me, I haven't felt full for a long time."

Chapter Twenty-Eight

A few weeks later, Mary Agnes felt movement. It wasn't much, just a small turning inside her. The stirrings were her secret, and she didn't mention it to Auntie. My baby, she would whisper, my little baby.

Staying home, hiding inside became tedious. Eventually, Mary Agnes had read all of the old *Reader's Digests* and didn't laugh at any of the jokes. She was alone most of the time as Auntie worked as a nurse's aid, sometimes pulling double shifts.

To keep busy and to help out, Mary Agnes swept the floors, scrubbed the toilet, cleaned out the fridge, throwing away the wrinkled carrots and the hardened government cheese. The fridge still had a strange smell, and she trudged to the grocery for a box of baking soda.

It was a warm day so she left her coat at home. Instead, she pulled her old jeans out of the closet, and luckily the oversize white man's shirt covered her belly. Knowing she might run into someone she knew at Buttrey's, she took the long way around to Green Front Grocery. Ducking through alleys, she avoided cars and the high school.

Bad luck. Gail was working behind the counter. "Hey, Mary Agnes, is that really you?"

"Hi," Mary Agnes said softly.

"Heard you got sent home. That you were a bad Indian."

"Yeah." She hung her head.

"I've had some bad luck, too." Gail pulled her lips to display her gums. "Lost my front teeth in a car crash." She stared at her friend's tummy. "Actually, I'd rather be toothless than knocked up."

Mary Agnes backed to the door. She could get the baking soda later.

"Hey, why don't you come down to the bowling alley? The gang meets there for a few beers. Wanda usually comes."

Mary Agnes shook her head. Seeing old friends was the last thing she wanted to do.

⤜⤛⤜⤛

Months later, Mary Agnes awakened in the middle of the night with a backache. It hurt so badly, she couldn't stand it. Instead of waking Auntie, she dressed and walked to the hospital. Each step was an ordeal. Her stomach was in a permanent cramp.

There was no one at the desk so she rang the bell.

"What can I do for you?" The night nurse seized up the situation. "Oh, follow me." She quickly checked the records. Hospital costs were covered for the Indian population.

"You are on the list. Follow me." She put Mary Agnes in the labor room with instructions to get undressed, into the hospital gown and into the bed.

Her labor progressed rapidly. She had never been to the ocean, yet pictured it now. Each agonizing spasm was a wave she let wash over her. There was no end and the wall of water struck her, rolled over her, and then left her helpless on the beach.

"Push," the delivery nurse ordered. As if she had any choice as her knees came up automatically. The loud groan she heard seemed to be not coming from her. Then a small bloody round thing appeared in the mirror on the wall, and the baby slid from her body. The nurse grabbed the infant and hustled it away. Mary Agnes fell back—it was done.

She finally got to hold her baby boy when they brought him for the first feeding. His face was red and his mouth open in a squall. His head was shaped like a football and he pushed his long legs into her stomach. She rubbed his squished head and told him he was a fine boy.

Mary Agnes and her new baby lived with Aunt Judy for just three months. Then Auntie left to care for her sister in St. Ignatius, and arranged for Mary Agnes and the baby to rent a room from her friends, Ben and Martha.

"Take care," Auntie had said as she left. "Don't drink beer or go to the bowling alley." Then she got on the train and disappeared forever. Mary Agnes had heeded her advice. As much as she missed her friends and longed for just one sip of cold, salty, foaming beer, she hadn't had a drink since she'd returned to Montana.

On moving day, she carried four paper sacks. Two contained diapers, bottles and baby blankets. Two held Mary Agnes's things— her every day clothes, a few pots and pans from Auntie, plastic plates and her school jumper. Why hadn't she thrown it away? Probably, she thought, because it was her last contact with Leo. She had written him countless times in her mind. Every day she composed a letter telling him of the warm Chinook wind the day she arrived, the sameness of the town, the train whistling in the night. However, she never told him about her growing stomach and the birth of her baby. He could get a job here, she thought as she scanned the want ads. They needed a mechanic at Jim's Husky.

Sometimes, she sat across the street and watched the train as it picked up mail and dropped an occasional passenger. Maybe he would surprise her, she'd whisper to the baby, and he'll step off the train.

"Here," Martha said as Mary Agnes arrived at their house trailer. "Put your stuff here." She pushed aside the curtain to a tiny bedroom.

"Your stuff will fit under the bed. The baby doesn't need a crib, he can sleep with you."

"Thanks, thanks so much." Auntie had promised to pay Ben and Martha twenty dollars a month until Mary Agnes could get work.

After her stuff was put away, Martha offered Mary Agnes a cig. Then she lit one for herself.

"Get me a cold one will ya, Ben? Mary Agnes and I have had a hard day."

Mary Agnes laid the baby on her legs. At three months, his head was nicely rounded. He had fine strands of black hair and his legs were getting longer. His sleepers were stretched to cover his toes.

"Christ sakes, Mary Agnes, get him some bigger pajamas. If you don't, you're going to stunt his growth."

Mary Agnes pulled on the fabric. "He's okay for now, and I'm looking for work."

Martha laughed. "Aren't we all?" She tweaked the baby under the chin. "Just another Indian baby without a father."

Mary Agnes pulled the baby to her chest, away from Martha's judgment. "He has a father."

"Right. Let's drink to that."

Mary Agnes reached for Martha's beer. She took a sip and then another.

The daily beer became a ritual. The women would sit at the kitchen table late in the day. They'd put their cigarettes on the green plastic tablecloth, and they'd open one beer at a time, and pour it carefully in the aluminum glasses. Mary Agnes's was green, Martha's blue. Purple was reserved for Ben if he got home in time and the red one was for company, which they rarely had. They smoked and drank and talked about getting jobs.

Chapter Twenty-Nine

"How'd you make out at the agency?" Martha asked when Mary Agnes had been with them for two months. "Any jobs?"

"Not today," Mary Agnes looked at her feet. "Can you believe it? They suggested a foster home for the baby."

"Your cousin Bonnie's dying to have a kid."

Mary Agnes jiggled the baby on her knee. "He's my baby! I'll get money from the agency in three more months."

"Not soon enough. We can hardly make the rent, and no more money has come from your aunt. Ben's testy since he got laid off. He popped me one last night." She rubbed her cheek. "Am I getting a bruise?"

In the next few days, Mary Agnes did her best to keep the baby quiet and out of Ben's way. The baby's colic persisted. She would dip her finger in corn syrup for him to suck. As soon as the crying started at night, she'd get up and take him to the kitchen.

"Hush, Fine Boy, let me rub your tummy." She'd walk him for hours and gently put him down when he finally fell asleep. Sometimes, she'd wrap him in an old bedspread and take him outside.

"Stars, Fine Boy, the same stars as in Nebraska. Leo could be looking at them. He'll remember the knife game. Your mom was good. One day we'll meet the train and you can be in a man's arms. He'll teach you to play basketball and I'll teach you the knife game."

The next morning Ben looked tense. His hair was greasy and he had a three-day beard. Martha was asleep on the couch. Mary Agnes had heard them arguing last night and a dull thud against the wall.

"I'm out of smokes. Seen any?" he asked Mary Agnes.

"No, sorry."

He pawed in the garbage sack and pulled out a few butts.

"Coffee?" Mary Agnes asked.

Ben held out his cup. "Can't you shut that kid up? He cried all night."

"Sorry, I'm almost out of formula. I'll have something coming from the agency soon."

Mary Agnes pushed a bottle into the baby's mouth. She'd watered the formula down with warm water to make it last. His lips closed around the nipple, then pulled away. He drew in a long breath as his face turned red. Mary Agnes put her hand over the baby's mouth. He squirmed frantically, and she let her fingers slip away.

His cries split the cold morning.

Ben, his face contorted, lunged at her with a raised fist. Mary Agnes scrambled away. She quickly stuffed the baby in her parka and hustled to the front step.

An icicle from the roof clunked on the porch. She kicked it again and again until it stuck in a dirty snow bank. Then she kicked the snow bank. The baby cried harder as she scrunched him into her coat. She was scared to go in. Ben could hit her; she didn't care. She wouldn't let him touch her boy.

Mary Agnes stopped as a car swayed down the ice-rutted road.

She retreated to the steps as the car parked by the trailer.

"*Ka-háy,* Mary Agnes. Remember me?" The woman's voice grated like radio static. She wore fur-topped snow boots and a long wool coat.

"No," she mumbled.

"Course you do. I'm Bonnie Sees Foxes, your cousin. We're in the same clan, Walks-with-the Moon. This is my husband, Carl, and we've come to help you out."

"No." She spit the word. "I don't need anything from you!"

"Is that the boy?" Bonnie came up to Mary Agnes. "Let me take a look." She opened Mary Agnes's coat.

"Carl, look, here he is. Where's the stuff we brought?"

Carl carried a paper bag. He was tall with a calm face and wore a fur-trimmed parka. "Give her the Luckies." He pulled out two cartons of cigarettes.

Mary Agnes didn't take the offering. She pulled her jacket tighter as the baby squirmed. Ben came out on the steps.

"I'll take those smokes."

Carl handed them over and pulled out his wallet.

He handed Mary Agnes two tens and Ben a twenty. "This should get you some groceries."

Bonnie held out her arms. When Mary Agnes didn't respond, she unzipped Mary Agnes's coat and removed the baby. "We'll get him new clothes. Carl got a crib yesterday and a high chair. I think we're all set."

Mary Agnes stepped toward Bonnie. "His name is Fine Boy."

"Don't worry, Mary Agnes," Bonnie said. "We'll give him a good home and you can come see him any time. Give him a kiss and hurry, it's cold out here."

Mary Agnes didn't move, her feet seemed stuck to the ground.

Bonnie hesitated and then turned to the truck.

"*Aho*, Mary Agnes, *aho*."

Ice crunched under the wheels as the car rolled away. Then it was quiet. She felt dizzy as if the earth had tipped. She wrapped her arms around her body, her coat baggy and loose without the baby tucked inside. Where could she go? She couldn't face the trailer without her child, and she never again wanted to see Ben's angry face.

She stumbled the few steps to the laundry building and slumped on a folding chair. How had it happened so fast? She was stunned. Had the social worker betrayed her or Martha? When could she get him back? And if she got him back, how could she feed him?

The machines whirred. The dryers warmed the cold room and steamed the window. Mary Agnes noticed things she'd never seen before. The old linoleum floor was covered with wet, muddy footprints. In the corners were piles of lint and dust. A cracked dryer door was mended with duct tape. One washer was missing the lid and someone had dumped their clothes in, despite the missing cover and water was sloshing over its sides.

Neighbors came in and out, shuffling their clothes between washers and dryers. As the afternoon faded to a pink-gray dusk, they left with clean, folded clothes in baskets and cardboard boxes. Nobody talked to or approached her. Her sorrow showed on her face.

Through the frosty windows, Mary Agnes saw Ben and Martha get in the truck and roar away, the muffler clunking on the rutted road. They had money for beer now. Were they celebrating the last of her crying baby?

At ten, the night watchman came to lock up. Mary Agnes felt too sad to move. However, she had no choice and trudged to the trailer. Her feet were frozen in her tennis shoes, and she stumbled on the icy path. The snow had stopped, the stars cold and bright, the

Northern Lights a green curtain on the horizon. She never looked up. *Her heart was on the ground.*

Chapter Thirty

1945

Mary Agnes sat at the kitchen table. She lit a cigarette and looked out the window. The sun sparkled off the snow. The ice was melting on the roof and made a steady drip, drip, drip onto the porch. The Montana winter was almost over, and she was excited. Ben was taking her to see her boy.

She bent over the kitchen sink and washed her hair. Wanda had been in the bathroom for over an hour, and Mary Agnes couldn't wait any longer for her turn as they had at least a two-hour drive. The liquid detergent was nearly gone, and she squeezed the bottle and got a few more drops. She soaped up again so her hair would be really clean.

"I got this book for him and a rattle." Mary Agnes held a wrapped package on her lap.

Ben gestured to the seat beside him, "You could set it down."

"Oh, no." She shifted the package closer to her chest. "I don't want to get the paper wrinkled."

"It's been over two years. He's not going to remember you," Ben said.

"The book is washable. The lady at the agency gave it to me."

Ben steered through the potholes and turned on to the highway.

"When is she going to get you a job? That's what I want to know."

"It's just pictures and letters of the alphabet. Is it too early to show him the ABCs and colors?" She touched the package. "Like they teach in kindergarten."

"You're asking the wrong person," Ben shook his head. "I didn't go and neither did my kids. We were too poor to buy shoes."

"Fine Boy will go to kindergarten. Bonnie works at the school cafeteria so they have plenty of dough. She could even send him to the Catholic School."

"That's not his name anymore."

"Who said?"

"Someone at the bingo game. Bonnie didn't want you to know, only us dumb Indians can't keep secrets." Ben turned on the radio. "Forget about it, he's not your kid anymore."

His hair stuck out like porcupine quills and his legs were plump and sturdy as he clutched the side of the playpen. He reached for Bonnie when Mary Agnes approached with the gift.

"Look here, you got a present." Bonnie said.

Mary Agnes knelt next to the wooden playpen. "Hi, little guy."

When she handed him the present, he grabbed the paper and crumbled it. Then he put a corner in his mouth. Bonnie lifted him out and placed him on the floor, and handed a clean diaper to Mary Agnes. "You do it, if you remember how. I do it all day, everyday."

She knelt beside him and tried to unpin his diaper. He looked at her, squinched up his face, and let out a loud cry. She tried to soothe him, but the cries got louder. Bonnie rolled her eyes and took over.

"I was afraid this would happen. Let's give him a minute to get used to you."

Mary Agnes sat on her haunches. She looked like she was going to cry, too. She unwrapped the package and handed him the rattle. He closed his tiny fist around the handle and shook it. The noise seemed to interest him, and then he pulled it to his mouth.

"Hey, that's about to come apart," Bonnie pulled the rattle out of his hand. "It's old."

"It was Grandma Lillian's," Mary Agnes said. "It's filled with sacred corn."

"You take it," Bonnie said. "He'd chew it open, but he can keep the book."

"Let him play with the shaker. I think he likes it." She put the handle in his fist.

"Watch him. I'm going out to hang the wash."

She shook it for him. "Here, Fine Boy, try it."

The baby took the toy and threw it across the room. Mary Agnes retrieved it, and he threw it again. Eventually he grew tired of that game and started to whimper. She tried to pick him up, and he wiggled away.

She saw a ball in the corner of the room, and rolled it to him.

"Roll it back, Fine Boy, roll it to your mommy." He fussed some more.

"His name is Pretty Weasel now." Bonnie stood in the doorway.

"Who named him?"

"My clan uncle."

"I have a clan uncle, too," Mary Agnes said.

"We did it last summer at the Pow Wow. We paid plenty for the gifts and the feast. What'd you do?"

Mary Agnes stood and brushed the crumbs off her knees. Bonnie opened the front door. "Ben's out front—you better go."

The sky had clouded up and snow was pinging on the windshield obscuring the view. Mary Agnes shifted in her seat. "When are you going to get the wipers fixed?"

"Aw, it's almost spring." Ben said.

"They gave him a different name."

Ben pulled into the Buckhorn. "Forget about him. Bonnie's his mother now."

"He'll always be mine!"

"I heard they needed someone at the dry cleaners. We can stop there on our way home and you can apply."

After a couple of beers, they forgot about the dry cleaners. Mary Agnes had taken the rattle into the bar, and she passed it around. Everyone gave it a shake, and Mary Agnes tried to do some ceremonial dance steps she'd learned from her Grandma. She stumbled into a chair and ended up laughing on the floor.

"See," Ben helped her into the truck, "things aren't so bad."

The next morning Mary Agnes slept late. Something nagged at her when she finally got up. Wanda and Ben were gone, so she couldn't ask them. Suddenly, she remembered. A job. A job at the cleaners.

She braided her hair and put on her parka. She'd hitch a ride to town. It was colder than she thought, and she sank her nose deep into the hood as she waited for someone to pick her up.

"Heard you needed someone," she spoke to Lloyd, the owner. "I can type."

"We don't need someone who can type," Lloyd put a bundle on the counter for a customer.

"I could wait on people. I know how to work a cash register." Mary Agnes added, "I can iron, fold sheets—I did a lot of that at the school."

"Can you work at night?"

"Sure, if I can get a lift."

"Come back at closing."

Mary Agnes stayed in town all day. For the first time in a long while, she had hope. The prospect of a job gave her energy, and she strode up and down Main Street. Then she ventured a few blocks north to the newer, nicer homes.

She watched a little girl in a red jacket and matching hat pull a sled. When the girl dropped a mitten, Mary Agnes ran to pick it up. The girl smiled and said thanks.

A teen tossed a snowball across the street at his friend and laughed when it fell short.

A new Pontiac backed out of a driveway, and the child in the backseat, his face in the window, waved to Mary Agnes.

How could she have a life like that? With a house, a car, and her precious son. A real life. Now she had a chance.

The smell of dry-cleaning fluid was strong. The air was warm and steamy from the vats of laundry and the mangles. The Polish women who worked in the laundry chattered in their native language.

"Give the office floor a good mopping, as well as the counter area. Clean the bathroom and sort the laundry. All the whites: sheets, pillowcases, white shirts in one pile and everything else in another. Oh, and clean the toilet and the sink in the bathroom," Lloyd said.

"Okay." She looked around for the cleaning supplies.

"Everything you need is in the back room. I'll come back around midnight to lock up and check the place."

Mary Agnes worked. She mopped, scrubbed the toilet and the sink. She even sat at Lloyd's desk and straightened the papers. About midnight, Lloyd came back. He inspected all her cleaning.

"Two nights a week," he said. "Saturday and Tuesday. I'll pay you cash so you won't have to join the union."

Mary Agnes liked her job at the cleaners, except things with Ben and Martha were bad.

"Ten bucks? That's all you can give me this month?" Ben fingered the wrinkled tens.

"Yup, I only got two nights at the cleaners."

Ben spit in the corner of the kitchen. "You gotta pay your way!"

Mary Agnes slumped on her bed. It was unmade, as usual, and the bedding smelled sour. She knew she wasn't earning enough, and she realized Ben was looking for a reason to get rid of her. Zipping up her parka, she left for work.

She slipped in the door of the dry cleaners. She was early; hitchhiking from the rez was not on a time schedule.

John, the presser, was still working, although everyone else had gone for the day. He had scruffy gray hair, a thin body and elbows that protruded like knots in wire.

"Can I sweep in here?" she asked.

He nodded and stepped on the pedal that released the steam.

"Watch out for the pile of clean trousers."

"Okay." She swept. It was warm in the room, the steam from the presser hissing and billowing each time he released the pedal.

Mary Agnes went into the bathroom and hooked the door. She needed to pee. The beer she kept in her parka was empty and she pushed it back into her pocket. She sat and the hot urine started and took its own sweet time. It felt good to rest for a minute.

"Did I ever tell you about Mexico?" John took a break and lit a smoke. He'd never talked to her before.

"Nope."

"The tequila made me crazy. I had a senorita, maybe more than one, some pigs and a shack on Rosarita Beach." John's smile surprised her. He was usually quiet and stern.

"What's tequila like?"

"Have you had whisky?"

"Sure," Mary Agnes said.

"Take whisky, add some lime, some rubbing alcohol, a worm, and slug it down."

Mary Agnes wanted a drink of tequila; she wanted it right now. Just then the back door opened, and Lloyd stepped in.

"John, what the hell—you should get off that leg. Don't want it seizing up again."

"We're done, boss."

Lloyd opened the cabinet door and gestured them over. "Cleaning looks good. Let's have us a little drink." He took a swig and passed the bottle. "That'll be your pay for tonight." Mary Agnes felt the wonderful burning in her throat and wondered if tequila could be any better.

In the next few months when she wasn't working, she stayed out of Ben's way. He was on her for money, cigarettes or beer. One night Mary Agnes heard Ben and Martha tumble in the door. She heard a scuffle.

"Stop it," Martha yelled, "you stupid Indian!"

"Who you calling stupid?"

Then she heard someone bang into the kitchen table. Martha grunted, scrambled into the bedroom, and slammed the door. When the steps came in her direction, Mary Agnes pulled her dresser to barricade the door. Most of the night she lay on her bed, completely dressed, ready to crawl out the window if she needed to.

Mary Agnes and Martha sat at the kitchen table the next morning.

"You got a place to go?" Martha asked.

"You know I don't." Mary Agnes emptied the ashtray. "Don't see how I could pay Ben more as I'm only working two nights a week. Cleaning is the only job I can get."

"What about your stash?"

"How'd you know?"

"Guessed."

"Has he been in my room?"

"Not yet."

"I want to visit my boy and take him something nice."

"Christ sakes, Mary Agnes, he's five. He's forgotten about you."

Mary Agnes looked stunned. Five years, it didn't seem possible. She still pictured him as a baby with the spiky hair and big eyes.

"We're hurting. Ben's turning mean, in case you haven't noticed. He said we could get twenty-five bucks a month for your room."

"What about your lease money?" Mary Agnes asked.

"Gambled. All gone."

They sat in silence. Mary Agnes pushed her empty beer can in circles. "I'm going to move to my grandmother's place. It's just a shack on the rez. The other day, I took a look at it, and with a little fixing up, it could work."

In a week, Mary Agnes settled in. For now, she had a place of her own. Her bed was piled with old quilts she'd picked up at the agency. On the shelves, near the sink, she had a box of saltines, two cans of beans, candles, matches and her toothbrush in a glass.

On workdays, when she finished at the cleaners, she stayed at the bar until it closed. She'd hitch a ride to get home, but at times, it was getting light by the time she got there.

She'd clean a little and rearrange her scant supplies on her days off. By afternoon she'd be thirsty and take her fishing stuff and beer to the river. She'd tie a string to her six-pack and float it in the cold water. Then she'd park herself on the bank where she felt safe curled into the roots of the cottonwood tree.

Once in a while, Ben and Martha stopped by. They always brought beer. If they caught any fish that day, they'd dip them in cornmeal and cook them over the fire out back. Many mornings Mary Agnes would wake up on the ground by the spent coals. She'd try to remember if Ben and Wanda had been there. She'd count the beer cans. If there were more than twelve, she knew she'd had company.

"It's Wednesday. Where were you last night?" Lloyd's voice sounded rough as he grabbed Mary Agnes's arm.

She felt sweat prickle her armpits. "I couldn't get a ride."

"Miss another day, and I'll fire you."

She went on about her job. Sure Lloyd might can her, then who was going to do the shit work? Not the Polish ladies, not the presser, not Lloyd, who lived on the north side of town—where the streets were paved and folks had grass in their yards.

Two weeks later she missed work again. Tuesday afternoon Martha and Ben had stopped over.

"Mary Agnes, meet Marvin."

She looked his way from under her hair. In no way did he resemble Leo.

"Marvin works at Texaco. He is living with us for a while."

"I've got to leave for work soon," Mary Agnes said. This felt like a fix-up, and she'd already told Martha she didn't feel like meeting guys.

"Don't sweat it." Ben looked at his watch. "We can't stay long."

Mary Agnes brought some saltines from the house. It was all she had in the kitchen. Ben produced a mason jar of chokecherry wine. The color was a rich purple and dark sediment lay in the bottom. He also had a sack of beer.

They sat in the back yard and drank. Carefully pouring the

precious wine in coffee cups until it was gone. Then starting on the beer. "Tell us about the Indian school in Nebraska," Martha said.

"Nothing to tell."

"Isn't that where you met Pretty Weasel's dad?" She laughed. "Your lips are purple," she said to Mary Agnes.

"So are yours!"

"We're going to take a walk." Martha pulled Ben to his feet.

Mary Agnes couldn't think of a thing to say. She drank as fast as she could and tried not to burp. Marvin just sat there like a bump on a log.

Ben and Martha were gone for a long time. Then they sneaked up and jumped out at them.

"Mary Agnes can throw a knife," Ben said.

"Got your knife?" Martha asked. "Show us how."

"No." Mary Agnes was getting sleepy. She'd been leaning against a log, and it felt really comfortable. For one minute, she closed her eyes. Next thing she knew, it was dark. The moon shone brightly, the night sky full of stars. Everyone was gone, and she'd missed work again.

"Here's your dough." Lloyd handed her fifteen dollars.

Mary Agnes knew from the look on his face. She took the money. Might as well get a drink, she thought as she trudged to the Montana.

The next day she went nowhere. She had a few supplies, some beer, beans and molasses, and in the far corner of the shelf she found a dusty jar of chokecherry jelly. She made the grubstake last for several days and then she had to go to town.

That night she sat on the bench outside the train depot. About eight o'clock a freight train rumbled by, seventy-two cars long. She ignored her stomach growling, and tried to sleep. By five a.m. she was starving. She crept around the back of Johnny Café and kicked away a dog that was rummaging in the garbage. She found some moldy bread and an almost empty jar of mustard. She took her booty back to the bench.

"Waiting for the train?"

Mary Agnes couldn't believe the nicely dressed white woman was talking to her.

"Cat got your tongue?"

"I slept here last night after I got fired."

"What kind of work did you do? Are you from the reservation? By the way, my name is Mrs. Henderson."

"Mary Agnes." She smoothed her hair and sat up straight.

"Can you clean?"

"Yes, I can type, iron, fold laundry, and wash dishes, just about anything."

"My cleaning lady just quit, and I need someone quickly! I've got company coming. My Caddy's over there." She pointed across the street.

Mary Agnes scrambled to follow her.

Chapter Thirty-One

1958

"Ouch!" Mary Agnes exclaimed. "That hurt!" A guy rammed her with his elbow as he pushed his way to the men's room at the back of the bar. He already had his zipper down. That brought her to the present, and she gazed around the bar like she'd been gone. Ben and Martha had left, the buzz was lower, and she was still waiting for the ten o'clock meet.

The serious drinkers leaned on the bar, their hats pulled low and their jeans lower. More skin was showing than anyone wanted to see. Beer and a burnt smell hung in the air. She sensed danger. Was Old Coyote behind this? She wanted a beer, and more than one.

The Caddy fishtailed on the snowy street. Mag laughed and Lois cringed. "Jesus, Mag! Slow down!"

"Don't sweat it, we're almost there." Mag's cig bounced between her red lips. "So the word's out about your paramour. Think Coach heard it?"

Lois rubbed the foggy window with her gloves. "*Don't* call him my paramour!"

Mag guffawed. "What else would you call a married woman's lover? By the by, where's Bobbi? She wasn't at the shop today."

"Church retreat, and Marlene's at a slumber party," Lois said.

"Good, we don't want the kids eyeballing us."

"Actually, something odd happened. Yesterday, I ran to the beauty shop for a quick do. Patsy said Bobbi was very troubled."

"About what?" Mag asked.

"Fighting with her friends, or who was going to drive the teacher's car."

"Must be the convertible." Mag closed the ashtray. "Godfrey! Cars and teens!"

"And one other thing, Bobbi's got a boyfriend on the basketball team. It's more like a crush," Lois said.

"Who? Could she have the hots for Pretty Weasel? She was so impressed with him when we went to the rez," Mag said.

"He only has eyes for me!"

The car slipped through the silent streets. The wipers struggled to move the heavy snow from the windshield. Small flakes drifted in between the windows and the canvas top.

"Hot Damn! Snow in April." Mag chuckled. "Just what we want for a rendezvous."

Lois pulled her collar up to her ears. "I'm freezing!"

"Poor you. Forget the cold and get yourself out of this mess."

Lois used her teeth to pull off her glove. "Now my stupid gloves are wet! What should I say to him?"

"It's your party."

"Aren't you forgetting you put me up to this?" Lois slapped Mag's shoulder lightly with her wet glove. "You need some fun, you said! Let's go to the reservation. Let's meet him at the bar." She slapped Mag harder.

"Okay! Okay!" Mag fended off the soggy weapon. "I'll give you that, only you took it too far!"

Lois rubbed her cheeks with her cold hands. "Was I crazy to get into this?"

"In the beginning, he used you to make the team. You needed a romp, and he's a horny high school kid. Did I mention *handsome as hell?*"

"When was the last time someone kissed your neck and said you smelled like peaches?" Lois asked.

Mag sneered. "You're kidding yourself. It's only a fling."

"Maybe. But it was something just my own." Lois's voice broke. "Not for the girls, not for Coach, just for me!"

The Caddy slid to a stop behind the bar. "When he comes, tell him it's over," Mag said, "and make it fast!"

⋙⋘

Mary Agnes couldn't stand waiting in the bar any longer. It was ten on the dot. She pulled on her parka and went outside. Standing by the bank, she had a good view of the alley.

Mag's car turned in.

Would Pretty Weasel show?

She could hardly breathe. Something bad was going to happen here. What should she do?

From out of the past, she heard Grandma Lillian's voice. It pushed her to movement. Stomping her feet in a Crow traditional dance, she called for Old Woman's Grandchild, the Sun's son to save him.

"Sun, Star, Sun," she sang. "Come to us, Sun, Star, Sun."

"Eii-hi-yi, eii-hi-yi." She continued singing and praying, leaving ever widening circles of footprints in the snow. Tired, she stopped and just watched.

Snow silently drifted in the beams of the headlights, exhaust puffed from the rear of the Caddy as it slid to a stop. Nothing moved. The snow muffled the street noise, and the minutes passed slowly.

Mary Agnes kept out of sight, hoping this meeting would end

the craziness. End it before Pretty Weasel got kicked off the team.

Through the white curtain of snow the Buick pulled up by the waiting Caddy. The two cars sat side by side like lovers on a blanket, waiting to begin the end. Then the door of the Caddy opened, and Lois dashed to the Buick.

Like a shot, a station wagon skidded through the alley and swerved to a stop. Coach leaped out, rifle in his hand. He jerked open the door of the Caddy, yelling, "Where is she? Where's my wife?" Then he crossed to the Buick and pulled the door handle. It was locked, and he pounded on the closed window.

"Open the damn door, Lois. Open the door!" He tried the driver's side, glaring at the lovers, and that door was locked, too. Then he banged his fist on the hood of the car. "Open up, you cowards!"

When they didn't, he cursed loudly and jumped up and down on the back bumper, violently rocking the car on its springs.

Mary Agnes ran from the alley and tugged on his jacket. "Stop it! I'm calling the cops!"

He shoved her down in the snow. He circled to the passenger side and thrust the butt of his rifle through the window. Glass sprayed everywhere.

Lois screamed, "You bastard!"

From the driver's side Pretty Weasel jumped out, leaped over the hood and tackled him. Coach fell to the ground, knocking his hat off. Lois grabbed the hat and held it to her chest.

Both men slid in the snow, pummeling each other and grunting. Lois and Mag clutched each other's arms. Mary Agnes leaned over the fighters, flailing her arms and sobbing.

The men scrambled and swore as they tried to hold each other down. Pretty Weasel landed a solid punch. Coach's nose spurted blood.

Coach got the rifle and pointed it, and then Pretty Weasel wrestled it away and crawled toward his car. Coach grabbed his foot, pulled off his loafer and tossed it away. Then he leaped on Pretty Weasel's back.

They rolled, first one on top, then the other. No one could win. It went on and on, snow dusting the fighters, as they made wide smears in the drifts.

From the pile of limbs, the rifle whirled away from wet fingers, pointed skyward, fell, bounced and fired. The blast sliced the air. No one could see who fired the gun or who got hit.

Mag ran to the bar, yelling, "Call an ambulance, get the cops!"

Slowly, Coach got to his knees, and stood as blood streamed from his face. Pretty Weasel stayed down. He grabbed his leg and moaned as his blood trickled like spring snow melt.

In the distance, a siren howled.

Just then, Rita, Donna and Bobbi screeched into the alley. Their headlights illuminated the shocking scene. Coach, Lois, Mag stood knee-deep in snow. Mary Agnes huddled on the ground, Pretty Weasel's head in her lap.

The siren gave a last *wop, wop* as the cops arrived. Their rotating lights turned all the white snow, white faces, and white light to red.

Chapter Thirty-Two

Two weeks after the shooting, Patsy sat outside on the trailer steps, skirt tucked under her legs for warmth. She loved to watch the silver highway curving into the darkening sky.

She felt so bad for Bobbi, and she wished that she hadn't been so wrapped up in her own worries. It was hard to believe that Lois Vernon had been carrying on with Pretty Weasel.

God-dammit it all, why did women get so desperate for men's attention? She was just as guilty as the next, lusting after Coach, a married man.

When Bobbi arrived for work, Patsy gave her a hug. With Bobbi near tears, she coaxed her to talk. She spilled the sordid details of her trip with the teacher.

Patsy gently touched Bobbi's shoulder. "I knew something was going on with that teacher and her car. Only I didn't realize that she'd played you against your friends. And I never would have imagined what she did to you in the motel."

"Yeah, that stupid convertible! All I wanted was to drive, and I ended up trapped with a drunk." Bobbi shuddered. "Only you, Rita and Donna know about the fingers and the tickle thing. I was *way* too embarrassed to tell my parents." She cradled her elbows to her chest. "I feel sick when I think about it."

"Don't worry. I wouldn't be in business if I gossiped. Does the school board know? That woman should be jailed!" Patsy gave her hair a touch of hair spray. "Bobbi, are you okay? A sick pervert has molested you. I'd like you to get examined."

Bobbi tugged on her bangs. "I'm fine."

"Let me know if you have any problems. We can go out of town to see a doctor."

Bobbi blushed, imagining a doctor spreading her legs and touching her down there. She changed the subject. "Do your ladies know about the shooting?"

"No one knows for sure who Pretty Weasel was involved with. Most everybody thinks it was Mag. And she's not denying it."

Bobbi jumped up. "*Seriously?*"

"Sitting right in that chair yesterday, Mag flashed a tiny smile when the subject came up. She didn't say it was her, and she didn't deny it when Mildred asked her point blank."

Instantly, the world opened up for Bobbi. Her life wasn't over! The total disgrace of her family was lifted. How was it possible? Mag? Only Mag could pull that off. "Is that really true? Why would she want people to think she was having a thing with a teen?"

"Loyalty to your mother, maybe, vanity, mostly she loves to be the center of attention. And her husband lets her get away with anything."

Bobbi wrapped her arms around Patsy. "Holy cow! What a relief! That changes everything. My devil mom is off the hook!"

"Yes, and here's the rest of it. The story is that the gun went off accidentally, so no one will be charged."

"I know dad is supposed to meet with the judge, not the reservation police, because it happened in town."

Patsy stacked the magazines on the side table. "Sounds like

everything will be decided behind closed doors, and completely
hushed up. They need your dad as a coach, and Pretty Weasel's just
another Indian who screwed up." Her forehead creased. "Too bad.
He was a good ball player!"

"I thought he was a knock-out. Now I could care less."

Looking in the mirror, Bobbi turned her head from side to side.
Her bangs were just the right length. She puckered her lips like she
was going to get kissed.

"So, did my mom tell you secrets? Like she and Mag were fooling
around with a teen-ager," Bobbi asked.

Patsy combed the hair out of her brushes. She scraped hard over
the trash and watched the clumps float down. "She didn't tell me
anything, only I sensed she felt neglected. That's why I gave her a
new hair color. She wasn't too open with me, but your dad mentioned a problem with you."

"Like what? When did you talk to him?"

Patsy paused in midstroke. "He came here to ask about a job for
you, to keep you busy, and I saw him at a get together at the lake.
Then, I ran into him at the Johnny Café one morning." She decided
not to mention the talk she'd had with him in the shop.

Bobbi's voice broke as she fought back the tears. "I heard about
the lake party and the dancing. Crap, do you have a crush on him? I
can tell you he's not that kind of person!"

"Bobbi, listen!" Patsy put her arm around her. "I've been getting
late night phone calls since I moved here. The caller wouldn't say a
word, then hung up. I have some things in my past to worry about. I
couldn't sleep, so I went for coffee early at the Café and bumped
into your dad. We talked."

Bobbi shook off Patsy's arm. "That better be true. I hope he's
not flirting with you to get back at mom."

"He seems like a family man to me."

"Did you think it was *him* calling you, for God's sake?"

"No, I didn't, although I was plenty scared. I've had a run in with an evil guy." Patsy smiled. "Anyway, forget about that. Now, I know who was calling. And I can tell you, I'm pretty happy with it!"

Bobbi looked at her watch. "Glad someone's happy. I have to be home by five on school days, nine on both school nights and weekends! And," her chest heaved, "I have to see the judge on Thursday!"

≫≫≻≺≪≪

After Bobbi left, Patsy glanced in the mirror. For once, she was satisfied with her face. The bags under her eyes were gone. Her cheeks were flushed, and her hair looked sleek and shiny. The source had to be the call last night. Her hand had trembled as she reached for the phone. This time she'd be firm, threaten to call the police if it continued.

"Hello," she'd said. "For God's sake, who *is* this? Can't you leave me alone?"

A throat cleared. "Guess I can't. I've tried, God knows I've tried!"

"Ord, *my good God*, is that you?"

"Yes."

"It was *you*? I've been scared to death by those calls!"

"I'm sorry. Sometimes I just wanted to hear your voice—other times I couldn't bring myself to talk." He sobbed quietly. "So sorry I frightened you. Can I see you? I owe you some money."

Patsy was elated. Like she could finally breathe. He wanted to see her, although she'd lied to him about the baby.

"Oh, Ord. It's good to hear your voice. What's this about money?"

"I've finally sold the house. Half is yours."

"Really?" She instantly thought of her loan. "I could use it!"

"Okay, then. Let's get together."

"When?" A flush of heat rippled through her body. "I can't wait to see you!"

Chapter Thirty-Three

T he snow had melted, and more was expected. After all, it was northern Montana. It was now three weeks since the shooting. The girls were crammed in the front seat of Rita's car. The air was smudgy with smoke, and the ashtray spilled gum wrappers and cigarette butts. They'd been cruising Front and Second Street for hours.

Rita turned in at High Hat Drive-in. "Who's getting a pizza burger?"

"Me and Donna. Root beer floats, too," Bobbi said.

"Who's paying?" Rita leaned out the window as a voice on a scratchy speaker asked for their order.

"I'll pay," Bobbi said. "I'm in such a good mood now that Bauer's in big trouble. But I can't shell out for the floats. I'm saving up for a new skirt to wear at next weekend's dance party."

"Any chance your curfew will be lifted for the night?" Rita asked.

"Maybe. Things are quieter at home now that people think it was Mag with Pretty Weasel. And remember, that it actually *was* my mom is a serious pinkie secret!"

"We got it!" Rita and Donna chanted.

Bobbi pointed skyward with her finger. "Pray for me! I have to see the judge on Thursday."

"After we eat, let's go to the church and light a candle for you," Rita said. She was the Catholic. Bobbie gave her a thumbs up.

They stopped in the parking lot to eat. Rita left the motor running for the heat. They unwrapped their pizza burgers. The sauce ran out of one, and they scrambled to contain it before it made a sticky red mess.

"Hey, look, there's Mick and Dave." Donna poked Bobbi with her elbow, whispering, "Wave."

The boys parked next to them.

Rita rolled down her window while Bobbi and Donna squared their shoulders and opened their jackets to give the boys a peek.

"Hey," Mick asked, "what's up? Heard Bobbi stole a teacher's car."

"Got it up to one hundred ten on the straight-a-way," Bobbi said.

Dave ran his comb through his ducktail. "Heard Bauer got canned."

"Yup." Bobbi wiped her mouth with her napkin.

Dave reached in the window and grabbed a handful of French fries. Rita slapped his hand away. "Stop it," she said, smiling sweetly.

Mick delivered the news flash. "Did you know that Miss Bauer crashed her car last week?"

Bobbi hadn't heard that. "Really?"

"On the Nashua Highway. She didn't get hurt or nothing. Lucky."

"She was such a geek! I'm glad she wrecked her car!" Rita said.

Dave took a swig of Coke and belched. "Another sub in English for the rest of the year."

Rita spooned ice cream from her float. "I love subs! They're so stupid, you can tell them anything!"

"See ya around, party at Cleveland's farm on Saturday night." Dave peeled out of the parking lot.

"Wasn't that the most?" Rita asked. "Mick and Dave have never talked to us before. They're *seniors!*"

"Yeah, Bobbi. Thanks." Donna made a smooching motion to Bobbi. "The kids think you're cool for stealing Bauer's car!"

"Me? Cool?"

"You've got to play it up." Rita crumpled her burger wrapper and tossed it out the window. "I'm going to pass a rumor that you drink Jack Daniels!"

Chapter Thirty-Four

Mary Agnes nursed her tomato juice. It was four in the afternoon, and she was the only customer in the Montana Bar. The bartender napped in the back booth with the newspaper over his face.

It was three weeks since Pretty Weasel had gotten shot. How was he doing? She knew he had a broken leg and was out of the hospital. She remembered kneeling by him in the snow, cradling his head, covering him with her parka.

It was the first time she'd touched him in years. She stroked his soft black hair and the pain in his eyes made her cry. He'd held her hand until the ambulance came.

When she'd whispered how sorry she was, he'd mumbled, "Truck. Red truck."

Could he remember her gift so long ago? It didn't seem possible. Had she heard his words correctly?

He was eight when she'd sent the gift. She'd never heard anything from him or Bonnie after. Wasn't even sure the hastily wrapped package reached him. She thought often in those long years about going to see him. How she'd looked stopped her—worn jeans, hand-me-down parka, dirty boots, and scraggly hair. No way was she going to show up at Bonnie's house looking shabby.

In those years, Mary Agnes had lived at her Grandma's place, and she'd hitched into town every day for her job at the dry cleaners. One Thursday, she stayed out of the bar, where she usually ended up before work. Instead, she went over to Ben Franklin's to get something for her boy.

"Can I help you?" the teen had asked.

Mary Agnes flashed back to her own appearance at that age, which was a far cry from this girl, who wore a pleated skirt, matching sweater and lace collar. Her white bucks were polished and her rolled socks matched her sweater. To top it off, her hair was shiny blonde and pulled into a smooth, long ponytail.

She asked again if she could help, and Mary Agnes noticed the braces on her teeth. Lucky girl, she'd end up with even white teeth. Mary Agnes remembered her black wool school jumper, her scuffed black oxfords, her crooked bangs, and her own front teeth that overlapped each other like ocean waves.

What if she'd looked like this girl when she was thirteen? Things would have been different. Instead of meeting boys behind the bathrooms at the park, she could have sat in a booth at the drugstore, and talked with boys whose dad's owned ranches and hardware stores.

"What are you looking for?" The girl followed her down the next aisle. Mary Agnes got the message. Indians had to be watched.

"Where are the toys?"

"Boys' or girls'?"

"For my son."

"What does he like?"

Mary Agnes felt a pain in her stomach. She didn't know what he liked. "What do you have?"

"We have the complete Roy Roger's Set. Two cap guns, gun belt and the cowboy hat. I'll throw in an extra roll of caps."

Mary Agnes touched the red box. Any boy would love cap guns. "Do you have a bow and arrow set?"

"We don't sell Indian toys."

"How much is the Roy Roger's set?" Mary Agnes asked.

"Only $5.95. Or you could get this wood burning set. It costs a little more, and includes a genuine leather belt he could burn his name on. See this scar?" She opened her hand. "You have to be real careful with the wood burner."

Mary Agnes shoved her hands in her pockets. She had two dollars and fifty cents. She couldn't afford either toy. "Got any trucks, something small I can mail?"

Mary Agnes grabbed a red plastic truck for $1.99. It came in a small box with a cellophane window. She pictured Pretty Weasel spinning its wheels.

In the trash behind the store, she found an old paper bag and used string. She had hurried to get to the post office before it closed for the day.

The sound of the bar door opening jolted Mary Agnes back to the present. She was surprised to see Bonnie Sees Foxes.

"*Kahaáy sho 'daache,* Bonnie."

"*Kahaáy.* I thought I'd find you here. I wanted to let you know Pretty Weasel's healing, and the doc said he could be back to basketball by the fall."

"I've been so worried. So he's doing okay?"

"He should be on crutches by next week."

Mary Agnes felt grateful and relieved, although she had a sudden urge to slap Bonnie's face. This was the woman who had pulled Pretty Weasel from her arms when he was three months old, the woman who'd seen his first step and heard his first word. For years she'd imagined Bonnie holding, bathing and feeding her son. Envy and resentment welled up in her like oil from sand.

She noted the changes in Bonnie. Her braids were gray, she'd gained a lot of weight, and she moved slowly, taking the stool with a small groan.

"I'll get a Coke when the bartender wakes up. Buy you a beer?" Bonnie asked.

"No, thanks."

After a moment of silence, Bonnie shrugged out of her coat. "I want you to know that Carl and I felt bad about taking Pretty Weasel."

"You never brought him to see me."

"We thought it would confuse him. Thinking back, I guess I wanted him all to myself."

Mary Agnes took a sip from her glass. "It was hard." Her voice broke.

"I'm sorry," Bonnie said.

Mary Agnes kicked the leg of her stool. She felt a small release when Bonnie apologized. And from the deep lines on her face, Bonnie had suffered, too.

"I *did* tell him about you. I never claimed to be his real mother." Bonnie's voice sounded shaky. "I said you loved him, although you didn't have a job or a decent place to live."

"You and Carl gave him a good home."

Bonnie fiddled with an old napkin left on the bar. "You only came to see him once."

"I couldn't come, you know that," Mary Agnes said. "No car, no job at times. You probably know about my drinking. What did I have to give him?"

The question hung in the stale air as they stared into the bar mirror. The bartender came by and asked Mary Agnes how her boy was doing.

"Ask her," she pointed to Bonnie. "She knows way more about him than I do."

"He's doing okay," Bonnie said, "if he stays off his leg."

The bartender nodded, got their drinks. He put a nickel in the jukebox, and Roy Rogers sang "Cool Water."

A few men drifted in, nodding to Mary Agnes. Talking of snowmelt and grain prices, they filled the stools, ordered beers and lit cigs. Bonnie coughed and waved her hand in front of her face. It didn't remove the smoke, just gave it a new resting place.

Bonnie broke the silence. "So, are you working these days?"

"I start a new job tomorrow." Mary Agnes said. "A dollar an hour and a raise in six months if I do well."

"So you quit the Hendersons?" Bonnie asked.

"You bet! Those white women made a hell of a mess for my *dáake*, for themselves, too!" She shook her head and her newly cut hair fell away from her face. "Mrs. Henderson even offered me a raise, and it was a good, steady house job."

"It must have been hard to turn that down," Bonnie said.

"No, thanks, I told her. I may be a broken-down Indian, with no laces in my shoes, but I'm not going to forget how you hurt my son."

"What's the new job?"

"Cleaning offices at night."

"Maybe you'd like to give Pretty Weasel something for college. He could go to Rocky Mountain in Havre if he graduates."

College? Mary Agnes felt a tiny sliver of hope. "So what about high school? He's dropped out here."

"Yeah," Bonnie said, "he could go to Buford. It's just a C school, but it'd be easier to make the team. They already have another Indian on the squad, Darrell White Owl. He's a beginning player, and not as good looking as Pretty Weasel."

"Those good looks got him nothing except trouble! Can you talk to him? About getting a fresh start."

"It's time we work together, Mary Agnes. He needs both of us."

Mary Agnes traced a carved initial on the worn bar. Patsy Cline crooned from the corner—mournful and sad.

What did that mean, working together? Maybe Bonnie wanted her help now, although she'd never contacted her over the years. No invites to his naming ceremony or his birthdays, no Christmas cards or calls when he had school events. It wasn't like she could just step in and be an instant mother.

"What do you want from me now?" she asked. "You never needed me before."

Bonnie pulled her coat around her shoulders. "I was jealous that you could have a kid and I couldn't. Carl and I tried for years. When the clan decided we should get Pretty Weasel, I was scared you'd want him back. Just plain scared."

Mary Agnes was amazed. How could anyone be jealous of her? She'd had nothing: no job, no man, and no help from the clan.

Just then a group of Indians trooped in and filled the rest of the stools. Bonnie grabbed her glass, Mary Agnes's arm, and they settled in a back booth.

"Okay. Say we'd be a team." Mary Agnes pushed aside her glass. "I don't know if he'd want me around. I haven't been much of a mother."

"For the love of Christ, you were only fourteen," Bonnie said.

"Will he talk to me?"

"He wonders about his father. Was it that kid, Leo, at the Indian school?"

"Yes." She lied. She knew *very well* who'd fathered Pretty Weasel, and it wasn't Leo. They'd only cuddled and kissed, and talked about the future when they got out of the school.

It'd been someone else who'd gotten her pregnant. She would never tell anyone *who* it was and *how* it'd happened.

Chapter Thirty-Five

1942

M r. Vanderweg had stood in the doorway that early January day.

"Need help?" he'd asked.

"Almost done." Mary Agnes yanked the last ornaments off the tree, and then started to unwind the lights. Nearly alone in the school due to vacation, she was spooked and scared.

"Let me help you take them to the attic." He grabbed the last box of ornaments.

The corridor was dark. Only a nightlight burned at the end of the hall. They started up the stairs. Mary Agnes gripped the boxes and climbed fast, Mr. Vanderweg behind her and breathing hard at the pace she set.

The lock, she thought, on the inside of the attic door. *I gotta get there first.* Bolted in, she could spend the night and come out in the morning when the staff was back from the Christmas break. Just before she reached the top, she stumbled. He caught her elbow and guided her through the attic door and, with a loud click, turned the latch.

"We don't want to be disturbed, do we?"

Mary Agnes held her breath as she looked for a way out.

"Nice in here, isn't it? The furnace duct blows lots of warm air." He switched on the single bulb hanging light. "Look here, it's our own cozy corner."

An army cot was shoved under the eaves. It was made up with a heavy green blanket and pillow. Her heart sank. She knew her ninety pounds would be no match for the large man. She rushed the door, anyway, to no avail. He was right behind her.

"You're mine now, Mary Agnes. All mine." He pushed her down on the cot.

She smelled the mothballs tucked in the blanket.

"What do you have to say to that?"

Nothing, she thought.

"Quiet, huh? Well, I'll see what I can do to change that."

Mary Agnes closed her eyes. She pictured her Grandmother's tent. The elk and the hunter painted on the side, her grandmother sleeping beside her.

He removed her shoes and stockings, and warmed her feet with his hands, stroking and rubbing them for a long time. Next, he worked his hands up her legs to the top of her skirt. She pushed his hands away, but he pulled her skirt off, and left her slip on.

"What a pretty slip. How soft on your skin. Feel it on your face." He wrapped the slip around his hand, pulled it up and used it like a washcloth on her cheeks.

Mary Agnes was in a trance. All through the harsh Nebraska winter, she hadn't felt this warm. She'd never been able to lie in her slip and not shiver. Her calf muscles knotted with tension.

She wasn't sure when Mr. Vanderweg slipped in beside her. His voice became like a song, a song she was familiar with except the words stayed just outside her conscious mind. The rubbing and touching went on and on. He massaged her arms, legs, face, and head. His fingers ran through her hair then ran through again, harder this time until her scalp felt liquid. With one hand he caressed her stomach. Holding her hands, he stroked each of her fingers again and again until they felt long, supple and soft. His hands were smooth and plump with no calluses to chafe her skin.

I hate him, she said over and over in her head, but her body said something else. It soaked up the warming, exciting touch. His hand lightly stroked her crotch.

Her mind searched for Grandma to save her. She smelled the smoky leather, her Grandma's sweat, the sage to chase away the evil spirits. She called out to her, *"Grandma, help me. Kill the white man—kill him with your hunting knife. Kill him now."*

But Grandma could not wake up. Her eyes stayed closed; she had already gone to the "land of the other-side people."

Mary Agnes saw again the elk, the hunter and the sun painted on the tent wall. The sun was outside the tent, then in the tent, then in her. The hand moved faster and faster until she moved too, her hips pumping and finally lurching into one final moment of melting, flowing looseness. The elk and hunter were in her, turning and flowing and bursting with yellow sun.

She awakened alone in the attic very late that night. The door was open, and the cold air from the staircase surrounded her. She moved her stiff legs, and then sat up. Her pink slip and white cotton panties were folded neatly on the floor. Scrambling into her clothes, she noticed dried blood on her thighs. She knew the matron wouldn't be back until morning. So she hurried to the dorm, slipped into her bunk, pulled the quilt over her head and cried.

"Leo's long gone," she told Bonnie. "However, he was a good kid and my best friend. We hated school and ran away together. 'Course we got caught and punished. Once in the dorm, we were telling Indian legends. Vanderweg sneaked up on us and was furious. He locked us out of the dorms, and we slept in the doorways, huddled together to keep warm. It was a December night, below zero. Two kids had frostbitten toes."

Bonnie touched Mary Agnes's arm. "I heard about the federal schools. It must have been awful for you."

For the first time, Mary Agnes felt someone understood. "It was terrible." She held back a sob. "I couldn't have made it without Leo. We met at the tire swing every day, and played our Indian games and basketball. And he set up knife games for me."

"I was never good at the knife game." Bonnie looked at her hands. She had a tremor and used both hands to pick up her glass.

"You okay?" Mary Agnes asked.

"Comes and goes," Bonnie said.

"Anyway," she continued, "I'll be happy to tell Pretty Weasel about Leo. And I have something for him."

She pulled a package from inside her coat. "Can you take a look at this?"

She carefully unwrapped a large book, which was covered with tanned deer hide and bound with thin leather strips. The book was titled *Crow Legends*.

"What the hell? Where'd you get this?"

"I made it, just for my son. Do you think he'll like it?"

Bonnie leafed through the pages. "You put a lot of work into this. Is it your handwriting?"

Mary Agnes nodded.

"It's beautiful! Where did you learn penmanship?"

"At the Indian school. Lots of times we had nothing to do. So we practiced our writing, the Palmer method. Over the blackboard we had a chart with all the lower and upper case letters. I used to show the little kids how to hold their pencils and practice the alphabet."

"It's a nice book. Who did the pictures?"

Mary Agnes smiled for the first time. "I did." She opened the book. "See my drawing of Pine Leaf? She was a Crow warrior."

"I'd like to read about her. We need strong women in our tribe. Heard of Freda Beasley?" Bonnie asked.

"I know that name. Grandma said my mom was hooked up with people working for our rights." Mary Agnes's tennis shoe slipped off and she retrieved it from the dirty floor. "It came to nothing."

"In any case, you can be proud of this book."

"I couldn't pay for better paper. It took me years to finish—I did each page over and over, until it looked nice and neat. I used Crow stories that Grandma told me, and I got the rest from library books."

Bonnie smoothed a wrinkle on one of the pages. "You got a library card?"

"No, *I* didn't." Mary Agnes grinned. "I sneaked Mrs. Henderson's card off her desk. I returned it before she noticed."

Bonnie laughed. "You're one crazy Indian!"

Mary Agnes tossed her hair. "I started out with *Old Man Coyote Makes the World*, because he was alone like me at my Grandma's old place."

She recalled the long nights when she drank beer and read the Indian legends aloud to the fire and to the pine trees. She had pictured her voice being thrust by smoke, up, up to the top of the dark green trees. And then the words scattering and falling, one by one into other's campfires.

"What other stories are in the book?"

"*Red Shield and Running Wolf,* the story of a brave Crow woman who married a Sioux, and the two tribes lived in peace for a long time. I wanted my son to know that different peoples could get along. Like the Indians with the settlers." Secretly, she hoped it would help her son with his mixed heritage.

Bonnie stroked her gray braid. "The whites never lived in peace with us. They just wiped us out with diseases and stole our good land! Why don't you come with me to hear Freda Beasley?"

"Maybe, if I'm off work."

"You could ask her about your mother."

"My mother left me with Grandma. We never saw her again."

"Well, think about it. How long did you live with your grandma?" Bonnie asked.

"Only seven years, although she taught me a lot. Her spirit was still in the gym when I sank the winning basket at the regionals. And," she continued, "there's a Crow woman, Little-face, who brought up her grandchild, too. Her name's Alma Hogan Snell. Alma went to a federal Indian school. She's writing a book." Mary Agnes drained her glass. "I'd sure like to meet her."

"Maybe you could be a writer, too."

"I'm no writer, although I'd like to meet one. Will you give Pretty Weasel the book?"

Bonnie put on her jacket and locked eyes with Mary Agnes. "You'll have to do that yourself. I'll tell him you're coming by."

Chapter Thirty-Six

1958

The windows in the judge's chamber looked out on the tall cottonwoods. Soon the buds would open, sending piles of cotton fluff along sidewalks and into yards.

With winter gone, it was a perfect spring day as the remaining snowmelt ran through the gutters. The men of the town gratefully removed the tire chains they'd used since September, all looking forward to a quiet ride on the paved streets and highways. The afternoon sun splashed a warm yellow path on the freshly waxed wooden floor of the courthouse.

The judge, clad in a western shirt with pearl snaps, sat behind an enormous desk. His silver spurs clanked when he nervously jiggled his leg. His eyes were weary as if he'd seen it all.

Bobbi, perched on the edge of her chair, sat between her parents. Going for innocent, she'd selected a pleated skirt and a pink sweater with a dainty lace collar. Miss Bauer sat on a chair in the corner.

No one made eye contact, and Bobbi felt like she had no allies in the room. She was afraid of Miss Bauer's ropy arms, hated her mother's guts and was embarrassed by her dad. He'd worn his sweatpants and around his neck was the ever-present gym whistle.

The judge cleared his throat. "Good morning, this is just a

preliminary hearing to see if formal charges are warranted." He glanced at his papers.

"Roberta Vernon, age fourteen, accused of car theft and driving without a license. You have some explaining to do."

Bobbi was scared shitless and her voice quavered. "Should I stand?"

"What do you have to say for yourself?"

Bobbi touched a growing zit on her chin. She felt like dashing out the door, until she remembered the bailiff stationed in the hall. Everyone was waiting for her to speak.

Swallowing hard and desperate for a Chiclet for her dry mouth, she began. "Miss Bauer, she's my English teacher, and I went to Williston, North Dakota, for a basketball game. She said I could drive."

"Did you have your parents' permission?"

"Absolutely not," Coach barked. "We said she couldn't even see ..." he pointed to Miss Bauer ..." that woman, except for class, let alone drive her car!"

Miss Bauer, her hair clean for once and dressed in a tweed suit, gripped the arms of her chair. The veins stood out on her bony hands. "She had her learner's permit."

The judge looked from one to another. "Miss Bauer, you thought it was okay to take a fourteen year-old overnight and across a state line?"

Miss Bauer straightened her glasses. One corner was taped, and they looked like they had been sat on.

"It was just a basketball game, and everyone goes out of state to play. As far as I knew, she had permission, and two other girls were going too, but they cancelled at the last minute."

"Did you think to check with Roberta's parents?"

Miss Bauer examined her ragged fingernails. "Bobbi said it was okay."

"I did not! You never even asked."

Miss Bauer glared at Bobbi. "You little shit. You stole my car and left me stranded!"

Lois whirled to face Miss Bauer. "Don't you call *my* daughter names! Setting your students against each other to drive your flashy car. What kind of person are you?"

"I'm a better teacher than you are a mother!"

Lois gasped.

Coach swore under his breath.

Bobbi sniffled.

"Okay, folks." The judge tapped his pencil like a drum roll. "Settle down! Give me a minute to think."

Coach and Lois turned their backs on Miss Bauer, whose jaw was set like concrete. Bobbi stared at her saddle shoes as if with one click they'd take her home like Dorothy's ruby slippers. The sky had clouded over, the sun gone from the floor. A cold draft rattled the window shades.

The judge gave his papers one last shuffle. "Roberta, to summarize, you and your teacher sneaked off to the game. Sometime during the night, or early morning, you left the motel in her car and drove home in a blinding snowstorm."

Bobbi wiped her nose on her sleeve. She felt like she was six years old.

"Why, in God's name, did you do that? Leave in the middle of the night and in a snowstorm. Did something else happen?"

Here was her chance to be vindicated—to tell the truth. She hung her head. Should she tell them? How could she talk about the rough assault on her privates to a man, even if he was a judge? How could she explain the heavy leg pinning her down?

"Nothing else happened," Bobbi whispered.

"Young lady, are you sure? You acted rashly and without thought.

This is your opportunity to help us understand why."

Bobbie held her breath. They would say it was her fault. And it was. *My fault, my fault* roiled in her thoughts. After all, she should have figured that Miss Bauer didn't want to spend time with a gawky freshman. There had to be a price for driving that magical car.

"Roberta?" the judge asked again.

Miss Bauer's eyes seemed to be drilling her back. She pushed the feelings down—no one could know of her sick shame.

"She gave me whisky, and I felt sick. After she passed out, I was afraid. I just had to get home. I'm..." Bobbi looked at her parents. "Sorry for everything."

"Whisky!" Coach stepped toward Miss Bauer and yelled, "Whisky!"

She shrank away.

"Get the hell out of town," he continued. "You'll never teach here again. Or anywhere, if I have anything to do with it."

"Your daughter is a sneak, and she owes me money for a tow," Miss Bauer defended.

At that, everyone began to shout.

The judge stood. In his cowboy boots, he was still shorter than everyone in the room, but his voice made up for his small stature. It could be heard in the courtroom, down the hall, out the door and down the street.

"Here is my decision: Roberta, your learner's permit is revoked for a year, and your parents can ground you, or whatever parents are doing these days. In my time, I'd have been belt-whipped!"

He pinned Miss Bauer with a hard look. "Miss Bauer, you're totally unfit to be a teacher. Thinking you could come here and prey on our kids. I strongly suggest that you stow your things in your fancy car and leave town. And don't come back, or I'll slap a kidnap charge on you that will land you in Valley County Jail, then federal prison."

He kicked the desk leg with the toe of his boot. "You people irritate me."

"Coach Vernon," the judge continued, "we're meeting later today on another matter. Now, everyone..." The judge motioned like a man shooing chickens. "...get out of my chambers!"

Chapter Thirty-Seven

Bobbi rested her head on the car window. The cool glass felt good on her face. Marlene slept on her side of the seat, and her mom slumbered in the front. The tires hummed on the wet pavement, and she read the Burma Shave signs. Driving to see her Grandma and Grandpa in Minnesota was what her family did every summer.

Thank heaven, they were doing something normal.

The school year finally ended, and she was glad. Her escapade with Bauer had given her some status, which she thoroughly relished. Stealing a car from a teacher was called "cool," and it allowed her to almost forget the shame of the rough attack in the motel. Mostly, she looked forward, not back.

"A high fly ball to left field," the radio was on low. "Going, going, gone! Another run for the Braves! And here comes Hank Aaron up to the batter's box." Aaron was her dad's favorite player. He slapped his hand on the steering wheel and said, "All right!"

The game seemed to go on and on. The sleeping, too. Bobbi liked being alone with her dad, while the others fell into a driving coma. She could smell his Old Spice, and she had the urge to burrow her nose into the short, bristly hair on his neck.

She liked listening to baseball, too. She was sick of basketball, and the weird feelings at the games. Most everyone in town knew something about the Pretty Weasel scandal. Bobbi sensed people shutting up when she was around, especially at Patsy's. The old biddies under the dryers continued to gossip about events. Luckily, Mag remained the number-one suspect.

Pretty Weasel's leg healed, although he didn't return to school. In fact, the team did okay without him. All the other players tried harder and the team went to State. They came in fourth, a good result for a small school.

Her mother and dad didn't fight as much now. Somehow, they'd patched it up. They spoke carefully to each other, their words like fragile china teacups. The old headboard started banging regularly again. It was all too stupid for Bobbi to think about.

She looked forward to her sophomore year when she could meet Donna and Rita in the green bathroom before class. It was the most important part of the day. Well, almost. Four o'clock, when the jail let out, was pretty damn good, too. And incredibly, her one big, terrible, huge worry was pretty much over when Rita said, "You're still a virgin, fingers don't count."

The highway rolled smooth and gray behind them, the car a mobile world of its own. The last thing Bobbi heard was the Hamm's Beer commercial, "From the Land of Sky-Blue Waters— Wa-aters." She pillowed her head on her arm, and she joined her mother and sister in the world of summer driving sleep.

Acknowledgments

Praise to Acorn Publishing for keeping me organized and making the publishing process manageable, also recognition to Laura Taylor, editor, for making small changes while maintaining the integrity of my story.

Kudos to my writing groups: The Bag Ladies, Coffee & Ink, and The Blue Moon Writers led by Scott Evans. Without their attentive listening, careful critiques and encouragement I wouldn't have completed this book.

Warm regards to fellow poet Gordon Preston, who long ago loaned me his prized IBM Selectric typewriter to publish my very first poems.

Many thanks to Anne Da Vigo who's been with me all the way and taught me "to be unstoppable."

Credit, as well, to professors David Merson and Harold Schneider of American River College, who patiently guided me through the short stories that later became my novel.

Also thanks to writing teachers Donna Hanelin and Les Standiford for expertly shaping "Chokecherry Girl."

I owe much appreciation to my daughter, Kjerstine, who has been my cheerleader and tech support.

I'm grateful for my Montana childhood where I was free to roam, play and develop my imagination. That small prairie town inspired many of my characters.

Lastly, I give a big thanks to my husband, Dan, for his constant love and support.